AFTER THE MESSIAH HAD GONE

After the Messiah Had Gone

Book 1: The Call

Robert Cole

Deep Thought Publishing
Spokane, Washington

Cover design by Neil Clemons
Map drawn by Rusty Lynd

ISBN: 978-0-9966640-0-4

Printed in the United States of America

Introduction

ON AN EARTH-LIKE PLANET in the Andromeda Galaxy, the Creator of the Universe skipped the introduction—and evolution—of the human being as the pinnacle of creation, opting instead for a new species of intelligent, social, conversant and powerful flying creature, the gull-hawk.

Frederick is a Commander of the 77th Wing, overseeing one hundred sixty-one gull-hawks for the Northland Flock. A respected warrior and leader, Frederick is rising quickly in Triumvirate, the theocracy that controls and guides the NorthLand Flock. Olivia sits on Triumvirate's High Council, bringing faithful strength and compassionate vision to the ruling body steeped in tradition and doctrine, now one hundred generations old. Frederick is also a burgeoning mystic. Unfortunately, mystics were viewed with suspicion and distrust by Triumvirate.

The High Council, concerned that Frederick's mysticism is threatening their doctrine and dangerous to the faithful, has ordered Frederick and his Wing put through the Call of Confidence, tested for strict adherence to orthodox Triumvirate creed and ways.

Complicating this turn of events is Frederick's budding relationship with Olivia, and his friendship with Joram and Dayleen, gull-hawks exiled years ago to the outskirts of the Flock.

A final, dangerous problem brewing is the bitter, long-standing conflict between Triumvirate and the Shahadah

Flock, ruler of SouthLand. The current dispute is over the Island of Eternal Peace, a sacred island lying between the two continents, a small sliver of land that both flocks consider holy, and both claim as their very own.

After the Messiah had Gone is a thought provoking, worthy addition to the oft-told "hero's journey." It is a story of faith, love, and war, and the inevitable conflicts that arise between those of differing viewpoints, longstanding traditions, deeply held beliefs, and hidden—and not so hidden—agendas. Will Frederick pass the Call, or will he fail, dooming his chance not only for glory within Triumvirate, but also for once-in-a-lifetime love with Olivia? Can Frederick retain his individuality, or must he forced to renounce his own truth? How does Olivia balance her leadership of, and loyalty to Triumvirate against her relationship with Frederick?

And what about the Shahadah Flock, who believe just as strongly as Triumvirate that their way is the only true way to the Most High? Will these two powerful, stubborn Flocks destroy each other in yet another bloody war?

Building on the diverse traditions found in Richard Bach's *Jonathan Livingston Seagull* and George Orwell's *Animal Farm*, Robert Cole has written a compelling, three-book tale that explores how someone with high integrity but unorthodox thinking and beliefs tries to live and prosper within a dominant, rigid theocracy. By weaving this age-old story within the context of a thinly veiled clash between the powerful faiths of Christianity and Islam, Cole offers profound, needed insight into our own world and the blind spots we all have, along with ways to bridge the seemingly insurmountable chasm dividing those of diametrically opposed beliefs.

After The Messiah Had Gone

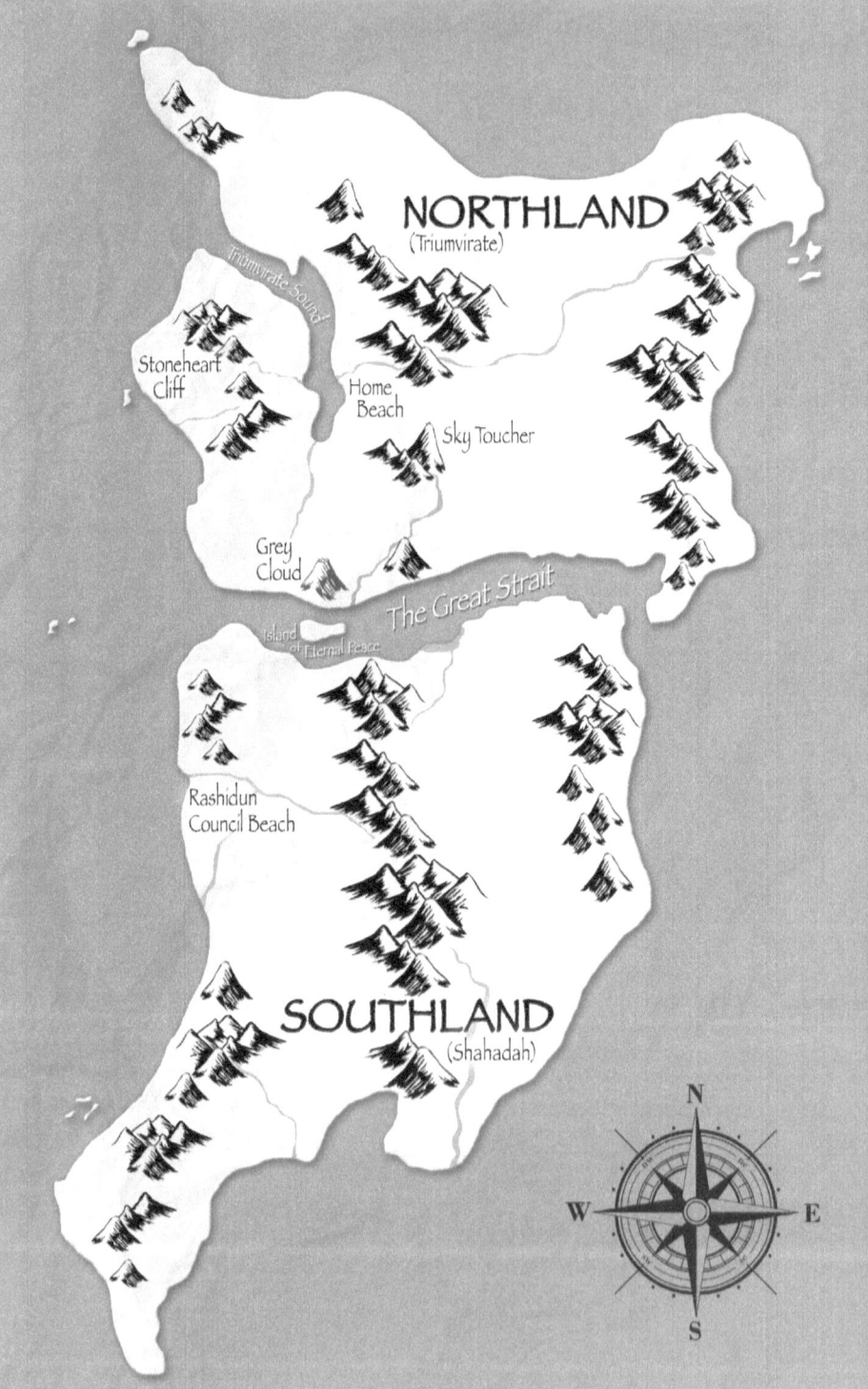

Prologue

Uncommon silence surrounded the Island of Eternal Peace, a strange, numbing presence that absorbed sound, and increased fear.

Uncommon because the Island was heavily populated with those who watched over—and guarded vigilantly—this treasured sanctuary. Uncommon since the Island lay in the middle of a churning tide-driven strait, with waves pounding tall, ancient basalt cliffs, in a relentless, boisterous rhythm. And uncommon due to the frequent wind gusts that whistled as they twisted through the thick stands of forested groves—pines, firs and cedar—which rooted on much of the Island.

This eerie, untoward silence unnerved Frederick as he approached the Island. Something was wrong, something serious.

Where is everyone?

Frederick turned back toward the sun—setting off to the west and obscured in a bank of clouds, oddly indistinct, fuzzy. The gull-hawk blinked, squinting hard, trying his best to focus on the sunset dropping down behind the cloudbank veil.

There were no gull-hawks, in fact no living creatures anywhere within sight, none.

Sudden movement off to the left brought his attention back to the Island. Another flyer soared in from the southwest, headed directly at him.

Friend or foe? Triumvirate or Shahadah?

The stroke pattern was not discernible, in fact unrecognizable to Frederick. He dove toward the Island, gained speed quickly while banking hard to the right, then accelerating before turning back towards the other one, still a mile away.

Frederick steeled himself for the inevitable fight.

Just before collision, the other, a beautiful white eagle-hawk—radiant and impeccable—wheeled about, calling out in words which Frederick heard, but without sound, somehow projected directly into the gull-hawk's mind: "Follow me, Frederick, follow Krystos, and find your deepest, truest self."

The immaculate flyer climbed high into the air, and Frederick took off after him. As he closed the gap, however, the pure white bird seemed to shimmer, and then disappeared.

"Hey!" shouted Frederick. "Where'd you go? And who are you?"

The words came out of his mouth strong, but hit the air muffled, deadened.

Confused yet fully alert, the gull-hawk circled the area, searching for the enigmatic eagle-hawk. As he looked northward his vision seemed to blur—the north cliffs lining the Great Strait had become hazy, colorless, a foggy gray.

What is going on?

These inexplicable happenings confounded the powerful warrior gull-hawk. He stared harder, but the north bank would not come into focus. *This is too strange!*

With nowhere else to go, he turned back towards the Island of Eternal Peace. He could land there, sort this out.

After all, it was the most profound sanctuary, the most holy place of all.

Oh no . . .

Although it was impossible, the sacred island was sinking, or perhaps disintegrating, but either way, it was disappearing into the Great Strait.

"No!!"

Right before his eyes, the Island of Eternal Peace slipped into the deep, blue water—every rock, tree, and living being who dwelt there was gone. No gull-hawks flew up—the sky was empty, completely blank.

The silence—uncommon and disturbing before—seemed to expand, growing oppressive, gnawing at his spirit. The gull-hawk scanned about, uncomprehending. And now the light began to dim—like it was being sucked away, depleted, and emptied into a vast, cold, infinite void. Frederick began to panic; his sense of being, of self, of identity was draining of everything he knew.

How is this happening?

As his own consciousness faded, he heard one final sound, a quiet whisper.

"Find your deepest, truest self . . . "

Chapter 1

OLIVIA'S EYES LOCKED on his as she came closer, her intent clear.

This could be it — our first kiss . . . .

Frederick reached for her — leaning forward, his heart pounding.

And woke up.

He strained to hold the wondrous, sweet vision of Olivia, so close, so beautiful, but no, the gossamer-like veneer evaporated, and much too quickly the images and delicious feelings faded.

Frederick closed his eyes and replayed all he could — seeing Olivia in a crowd, she recognizes him and comes over. When they are together, she approaches him, and what else? But the rest dwindled away.

What did it mean — was the dream just his heart's desire? Perhaps a portent of things to come? Or, something else — a clue about him, maybe from the Most High?

Oh well, he thought, *dreams are elusive — and it's time to get going.*

He shook himself, stretched his wings, and glided from his tree perch high amidst the deeply rooted grand firs to the river below for a cool, early morning drink.

The rising sun greeted the gull-hawk — reflecting in a glistening dance off a stretch of slow-moving water, the sun barely peaking over the eastern hills. *Another glorious sunrise,* thought Frederick, *if only there was time to appreciate it, time to actually savor the beauty of creation at sunrise with-out worry or thought to the future.* He sighed, *that time may be coming soon, if I can just get my request for leave granted!* "Heck," he said out loud—though no one else was near—"there I go again, putting off until later the moment when I'll enjoy something, never right here, never right now. I am so predictable sometimes."

Frederick landed on his favorite basalt rock, just start-ing to warm in the early morning sun. He took a deep drink, cold and quenching. The light breeze ruffled through his feathers, and he scanned the area, alert and fully aware. Here, the river flowed swiftly, cascading through a series of jagged boulders, creating a delicious roar, so familiar, and always welcome.

As he sat, another thought arose, but more urgent. His pulse quickened as Frederick once again pictured Olivia, the beautiful, the graceful, the powerful Elder of the High Council. The last time they were together for real, Olivia expressed genuine, heart-felt affection for him. *An incred-ible, once-in-a-lifetime moment. The birth of true love, perhaps?* He could almost live on that memory forever, and he shivered as the deliciousness ran up and down his body. The feeling passed and Frederick frowned, recalling how Olivia had to depart right after her intimate revelation, the full potential of their relationship unfulfilled.

He remembered everything from that day, now etched permanently in his mind. Their time together was always limited, given their demanding positions, and desire to keep their relationship private. Three moon cycles past, though, on a Day of Rest, they arranged to meet, and flew together for hours, enjoying each others' company, reveling in the joy of flight, and each other. The two stopped to rest on an old, half-burnt Douglas fir that overlooked a long river canyon. They caught up on their respective lives since their last time together, and then the conversation took a turn.

"Frederick, I want to tell you something very important. Okay?"

"You always have my attention, Olivia."

"Do you recall it was you who said that love will find a way, if it's meant to be?"

"I do."

"Well, love has found a way, deep into my heart. I think—no, I know—you are the one for me. I love you, Frederick."

Frederick remembered that he sat there on the top of that tree, momentarily stunned, but his heart raced, and his whole body filled with love and joy.

"And I love you, too, Olivia. There is no doubt in my mind how very special you are."

Since that day their respective Triumvirate duties had intervened and the relationship remained unfulfilled. Still, the possibilities and the potential for true love was out there, like the bud which requires only water, sunlight and a little time to bloom into a miraculous, scent-filled flower. Frederick felt his heart soar as his mind projected the two of them, flying together, just like this morning's dream, in synchronicity, in love. *Maybe,* he thought, *maybe I can get enough leave, and maybe, if the Most High wills it—and Olivia can break away from her responsibilities—maybe then we can finally be together, truly together!*

But today, as most days, Triumvirate duty called. The gull-hawk shook off his fantasy, and turned towards the west. Frederick took a deep breath, spread his wings, and launched upward, stroking powerfully to gain altitude. In a moment, he climbed high enough to draft the brisk wind currents common on these late summer mornings. Olivia's graceful form came to mind again, and a strong gust knocked the gull-hawk to the side, reminding Frederick of the deeply-ingrained flying lesson of keeping his mind on the present. Frederick made a conscious effort to shut off his constant, seemingly never-ending thoughts of Olivia, as it was more important right now to catch the strong northwestern coastal airstream. He stroked upwards until he felt the beginnings of that airstream. Opening his wings, he quickly reached the ocean, inhaled the pervasive scent of salt, and then sailed up the rugged coast, joining a few other gull-hawks in the pursuit of their first meal of the day.

The higher-ranking officers, commanders, and Elder gull-hawks had been allotted feeding grounds based upon their position in Triumvirate. While most of the regular gull-hawks forged wherever they could, a few, like Frederick, had earned the right to feed in a prime spot. After several years of distinguished and highly decorated service, Frederick was now the commander of the 77th Wing, with one hundred sixty-one Triumvirate warrior gull-hawks reporting to him. To Frederick's right, his second-in-command, soared in an intercept glide. As Gregory approached, he called to Frederick a good morning: "Wonderful day, isn't it?"

"Another perfect sunrise, another job well done by the Most High Commander-in-Chief of the universe," Frederick replied; then he altered his wing pattern slightly, banked to his right, and began to descend. "I'm going deep sea fishing," was all that came out as he pointed downward and dove toward the sea.

Plunging rapidly, Frederick adjusted his feathers to provide the trajectory needed to catch a fish he'd glimpsed rising to the surface. He struck the frigid water, closed upon his target and, a moment later, rose out of the bay using powerful wing strokes, breakfast secured in his talons. He let out the Triumvirate's victory cry and flew to shore to enjoy a succulent meal.

Breakfast continued until the sun had cleared the eastern horizon and begun its ascent into the cloudless, blue sky. Frederick and Gregory flew together to the Triumvirate Patrol assembly area, just up the coast a few flaps away. The gull-hawks of the 77th and 78th Wings assembled each day in the shadow of Stoneheart Cliff, a looming, massive stone seawall, named after a strategic battle won by the Triumvirate gull-hawk warriors in the last Great War, several generations past. It amused Frederick that the lower-ranking gull-hawks all called it "The Cliff," not being big on sentimentality, or history, having all been born after the war had long ended.

Gull-hawks in both Wings were already beginning to join up in formation as Frederick and Gregory flew at a rapid clip up and over the cliff's ocean-side edge. All twelve of Frederick's squad leaders, eight squads appeared to have their full complement of thirteen and the other four had almost all gull-hawks present. Frederick spied a contingent of gull-hawks approaching from the northwest; the group split up when it got close; eleven gull-hawks headed for Frederick's Wing—including the rest of the 77th Command Team—and the others flew to the 78th.

When the twelve squads were complete, they took off and closed to their standard attack formation. This time-honed, standard Triumvirate formation consisted of each gull-hawk and squad flying in the shape of an inverted-V. Frederick watched as they became, in essence, one enormous gull-hawk, climbing high into the sky, veering left, then right, then into another steep climb. Without warning, the squads twisted into a loop and descended downward, picking up speed. They banked sharply left, spread their ranks, and charged directly at their commander in an intimidation maneuver. As they reached the hovering Frederick, the twelve split into two, missing him by a mere wing's width. The groups merged back into one, pulled into a tight, rapid loop and turned back towards Frederick—and the Command Team. Frederick gave the signal to fall in, and the squads— one hundred fifty-six gull-hawks strong—flapped to a stop in a synchronous motion. They landed, as they did every morning, on a large rock ledge up high on the Cliff. Frederick let the updraft bring him to his Wing, gave the signal for all quiet, and began the morning prayer:

> "Oh Great Provider, Protector, Sustainer,
> You are everywhere;
> Your name is sacred;
> Your kingdom is come;
> Your will permeates the earth,
> even as it permeates the universe.
> For Yours is the kingdom,
> the power, song and praise
> from all ages . . .
> . . . and throughout all ages.
> We seal this prayer in love, faith, trust, and truth."

The gull-hawks of the Wing echoed their leader's words; then began the minute of silence, as each gull-hawk was required to still him or herself and become a vessel for the Most High. Those that needed cleansing, who were burdened by errors or guilt (there are always plenty of these), asked for forgiveness first. Krystos felt no specific guilt, but still submitted in his own way. *Krystos, I make mistakes every day. Please forgive any pain I have caused my fellow gull-hawks. Help me hear your voice, to love as you loved, and become the gull-hawk you want me to become.*

The silence of the gull-hawks allowed the swirling wind to be heard as it came off the sea and blew up and over the Cliff. Waves pounded the jagged rocks anchoring the Cliff where it met the water. Frederick marveled at this never-ending dance as he fought his own battle between thoughts and silence, the external world and that of the Most High. When the minute was completed, Frederick concluded:

"Love the Most High with all your heart, soul and mind,

And love your fellow gull-hawk as the Most High loves creation."

He took a deep breath, lowered his voice and spoke more of the sacred words:

"Make your eyes into one,

And your whole gull-hawk form

Will become full of holy light."

The morning ritual contained a second minute of silence, during which each gull-hawk once again committed to the Most High. The prayer Frederick just spoke was his personal addition to the morning ritual. Although it could be found within the Sacred Traditions, the words were from an obscure passage, overlooked by most. Commanders had a small bit of discretion here, so Frederick was not violating any rules. He wanted his gull-hawks to be totally focused when flying, and so imparted special exercises to the 77th and help bring their minds to "one point," the art of total concentration.

For one hundred generations Triumvirate had taught that surrender to and complete focus upon the Most High's son Krystos was the key to salvation, the way to the Most High, the path to heaven. It was taught that with Krystos, all was possible; but without the Son, well, difficulties multiply, and salvation was surely impossible. Frederick knew this, and knew how many gull-hawks had turned their lives around, found direction, purpose, and real meaning by following Triumvirate's teachings. Still, not all of the Sacred Traditions rang true to Frederick. There were a few important teachings that simply did not reconcile, did not ring true, and in fact contradicted what he had observed in his life. But Frederick kept those thoughts silent, deeply buried. After all, what did he really know; he was just one infinitesimal, finite gull-hawk? Plus, so many of the words of Krystos were powerful, piercing and righteous. In the end, Krystos's flying—as recorded by his disciples—well, he was the best to ever take to the air. Despite Frederick's doubts, there was no questioning the ultimate target upon which he wanted his charges to focus—Krystos, the messiah and wayshower of truth.

Right now, in the present moment, Frederick fought to quiet his own mind, trying to remember the Traditions. *It is so easy to say—our focus point is Krystos,* thought the gull-hawk, *but painfully difficult to reach, and then to maintain for any length of time.* He sighed, took a deep breath, and reached farther within, finally finding a tendril of peace, like gliding on a light breeze on a warm summer day. He, and the entire 77th Wing, where in the thralls of "giving up the soul" to the Most High, and Krystos.

The sun's penetrating rays stretched into the forests, rivers, hills and valleys, the light snaking over the land, illuminating everything. With the wind subsided, Frederick bathed in the summer's heat, feeling it warm his damp feathers, thankful for the sun's powerful energy as it finished the drying process from his breakfast dive into the bay. At last, all thoughts had vanished, and he sat at peace, silent, empty, for what seemed like a long, wonderful time.

"Ex-Excuse me, er, Commander, ah, the minute, or in this case minutes are up," whispered his second-in-command. Startled, Frederick emerged from his meditative silence with a shake of his feathers.

"Thank you, Gregory," Frederick replied while turning to his Wing. They looked back with respect, wonderment, and just a touch of bemusement, for all had noticed their commander's extension of the time of silence. Of course, this was not the first occurrence. These lapses had been repeating with increased frequency. Because of several previous out-of-the-ordinary occurrences, Frederick had acquired the reputation as a mystic among the Wings that patrolled up and down the west coast. While most admired Frederick's faith and deep connection to Spirit, there were a few who thought the 77th commander's behavior to be dangerous.

Frederick shifted his Wing's attention away from himself by launching into the morning lesson. On this particular morning he chose the saying from a very ancient section of the Sacred Traditions: 'Peace, be still, and know the Most High'. The Son of the Most High, Krystos, also known as Master, Lord, Savior, Messiah, and several other names, taught his disciples that to reach the highest level, one must remember that the Most High sees the perfection within each of us, even if we do not, and despite our imperfect nature. A true disciple must believe this fundamental truth with all of his or her heart.

The gull-hawk mind cannot comprehend the totality of the Most High, but by becoming still, can follow Krystos and—at least temporarily—merge with the Most High. Later Triumvirate evolved this potential to experience the Most High into the creed of giving oneself up to the Son, to be filled by the Most High's Sacred Spirit. Frederick preferred the original teaching, and while not heretical, was clearly unorthodox. None of the 77th Wing minded that, in fact, they were fascinated by these obscure, neglected teachings.

Frederick and the 77th Wing composed merely a small piece of the vast force of Triumvirate gull-hawks. Frederick had committed himself totally, as is required in Triumvirate, to protect the immense Flock that calls the NorthLand territory its home. And the Cliff area was his patrol, his responsibility. This thought washed through him as he once again spoke to his Wing:

"The morning comes as the sun rises
Morning comes in you as the Son rises
In the sky,
In the clouds,
in the mind, in the heart
Different, yet one."

The gull-hawk looked at his command team—Gregory, second in command, strong, faithful, practical, and always able to find a righteous solution to whatever confronted them. David, the immensely strong yet gentle conscience of the Wing, arguably the best flyer in the Wing and a minor mystic himself; his role was the Wing Commander's personal bodyguard. Nathan—the healer—who knew all of the healing arts, including the most important salve of all—unconditional love. These three, along with a messenger and recorder, comprised the Wing command team. Besides the six gull-hawk command team, each Wing was made up of twelve squadrons, each with thirteen gull-hawks headed by a squad leader. The formation of a Wing was thus patterned after Krystos, who—according to the Sacred Scripture—surrounded himself with twelve disciples. It was a very, very old gull-hawk tradition.

In keeping with Triumvirate time-honored practice, Frederick began to fly, beckoning the Wing to follow. He dove to the beach below the cliff, in-taking breath as the gravity force pulled him and the air pressure resisted. Frederick snapped into horizontal flight just above the beach, and let his momentum carry him up the shoreline toward one of the great sea rocks lining the coast. His command team trailed him, and the squadrons followed them, the leaders and experienced ones flying smoothly, those new to the Wing flying a bit erratically but always gamely. Nearing the largest of the sea rocks, Frederick banked left, out toward the sea, and then banked again, this time back towards the land. This was the first flying lesson of the day, just as it was the Master's elementary lesson given a hundred or so generations ago. When all had completed the maneuver, Frederick sought out where the breeze blew up a sloping cliff, and let the powerful ridge-lift carry him a thousand feet up with no real effort. Glancing backwards, he checked on his Wing's progress, and proceeded inland, searching for another familiar, recurring thermal. It took only a few seconds before he found the thermal's rising current, where air rises like a bubble which falls "away" from the ground and up into the sky.

The 77th commander rode the thermal higher and higher, banking tightly and flapping efficiently to gain as much altitude with the minimum exertion. He reached the thermal's upper limit and waited until the Wing joined him, all one hundred sixty-two Triumvirate gull-hawks. They circled in precise formation before following Frederick as he came sharply out of the thermal and sped back toward the ocean. Frederick soared momentarily while he judged the distance to the shoreline and gauged the crosswinds, then made the dive towards the sea.

Intense pressure pummeled him as he plunged earthward; his wings snug to his body. Adrenaline surged—a warning of the tremendous risk of high-speed flight. But he was a Triumvirate commander, and risk and speed and leading his Wing were what he lived for. Closing upon the shoreline at nearly two hundred miles per hour, he made the minute adjustments required, leveled off just above the water, and rode his momentum several miles out to sea. The Wing followed, most not quite as fast, yet just as determined and joyful in this type of flying. Soon they were back to level flight, skimming over the long, straight beach lying south of StoneHeart Cliff, headed north, to their base.

A quintet of gull-hawks appeared out of the clouds, in the formation of official High Council communication. Their approach was in itself unusual, for the routine throughout Triumvirate deemed that *all* gull-hawk Wings were undergoing their flight training at exactly this time of the day. And no lesson was to be interrupted without urgent reason.

One of the five gull-hawks flew slightly ahead of the other four, indicating he would deliver the High Council's message. The other four were rarely seen, elite warrior gull-hawks, specially trained within Triumvirate to be ferocious fighters. The fifth gull-hawk was actually more powerful—at least politically—for he was a High Council Messenger, and the other four always obey the Messenger they escort—always. The Wing's mood switched to nervous curiosity, clearly anxious about what this communication was to be, their sense of well being washed away, gone.

This can't be good. Frederick's heart began to pound. Something wasn't right; he felt twisting in his stomach, a remorseful twinge in his heart.

What have I done?

Frederick brought his Wing squads out of horizontal flight and onto the beach. The Messenger landed in front of Frederick, and with no introduction, no greetings, began:

"According to the ancient laws of the Flock, as amplified by the Son, and perpetuated by Triumvirate, the 77th Wing will participate in a Call of Confidence. The Call will occur seven suns from today, on the day when the moon is absent from the night sky. As is our tradition, the Apostle will preside over the Call, and the twelve Elders will judge the performance of the Wing. Those who face the Call must search their heart and purge all wickedness, and remember the Sacred Traditions and Teachings. Make yourself as pure as possible—you will be judged for your flying ability, your teamwork, your spiritual progress, your loyalty to Triumvirate, and your commitment to the Most High and his son, Krystos.

"The Call is divided into two parts. The first part is the Test of True Flight. The second: the Test of True Faith. The details of each test cannot be told, or ever revealed by anyone who participates. But even though you may not know exactly what these Tests entail, and even though they are extremely rigorous—as difficult as any test or trial ever faced—you can succeed, if you've learned your lessons well, if you are a true Triumvirate gull-hawk, and if you can demonstrate your ability and your faith under the most intense pressure, and the closest, finest, truest scrutiny.

"The Call is a great challenge, a noble test, and you are implored to act accordingly. Many are called, but only the best, the most faithful, are chosen. Stay centered in the Son, and, Most High willing, you will pass. What lies on the other side of the Call is known only to the Most High." The Messenger nodded to Frederick, lifted off, and flew toward the outcropping of large sea rocks. His protectorate of gull-hawks shadowed him, picking up speed in time with their superior. The Messenger veered around, flying a true horizontal pattern, in exactly the place where he had interrupted the training. Frederick took the hint and rose to follow the Messenger in the eternal quest for perfect flight. In total silence, Frederick's Wing quickly joined their commander in formation. With very precise wing strokes, the Messenger led the way down past the long beach, the sea rocks, and continued on southward along the craggy shoreline. Coming to place where a river drained into the ocean, the Messenger broke the horizontal pattern, and headed east up the river valley, back the way he came, the four elite warriors trailing. Frederick led his gull-hawks on a slow, banking right turn, and the 77th rode the updrafts toward their assigned perch high up on the Cliff. His Wing instinctively adjusted their formation, and rode the strong ocean breeze just behind their leader. Landing in his commander's place, Frederick struggled to calm his soul. It took all of what he had learned to gain control over the trembling of his wings.

Most High, what am I to do? How am I going to survive this? Why are we being Called? And how am I going to maintain in front of my Wing? How can I lead them when I feel this way? Cutting off these negative, unproductive thoughts, he focused instead on his breath, feeling it turn, in and out. The effect was immediate—his tenseness began to quell, and the blood flowing through his veins slowed to near normal. The one hundred sixty-one other gull-hawks stood quiet, watching and waiting for Frederick. Even though nothing was spoken, three words were on everyone's mind.

"CALL OF CONFIDENCE!!"
"CALL OF CONFIDENCE!!"

The words echoed silently through every gull-hawk there, exerting fear and impending doom. They closed ranks in anticipation of Frederick's response. They looked up to him, respected him, believed in him, and needed their commander's strength, especially now. Frederick's Wing was to be judged, completely, totally, the ultimate judgment. Being "called" occurred only when the highest levels of Triumvirate had a serious concern about the inner workings of one of their Wings. Since the Wing Commander was in charge, there was no doubt that it was Frederick, as Commander, whose abilities were being challenged, who was under suspicion. Frederick knew, his squad leaders knew, the command team knew, and every squad members grasped that the Call for Confidence would affect each and every one of them—the entire 77th—both their careers and their lives. A negative judgment would carry a stigma, perhaps impossible to overcome. To pass the Call, the gull-hawks must fly at peak performance, and answer the questions impeccably. Frederick felt comfortable with his gull-hawks. He knew his Wing was deeply committed to the mission of Triumvirate, were tremendous flyers, and spiritually sound. Their only possible weakness was that they were fiercely loyal to their leader. No, it wasn't the Wing that Frederick was worried about. It was himself that had Frederick most concerned!

In another part of the great NorthLand controlled by the Triumvirate Flock, a day's flight away, twelve powerful gull-hawks stood in a semi-circle, facing their leader. The Apostle was the most powerful, the ruler of all Triumvirate, and a gull-hawk infallible in spiritual matters—according to the Sacred Traditions. The twelve, known as the High Council of Elders, were speculating about today's events, the Apostle silently observing. The Council's mood—a mixture of somber reflection and playful giddiness—had the Apostle concerned, quite concerned in fact, since he knew that a new chain of events had begun, with the outcome far from predictable. But he did not want his consternation to affect the others and so he watched, mute, in quiet communion with the Most High.

"By now the Messenger has surely informed the 77th of what is to happen to them," said Elder Jeremiah.

My messenger should have informed them several hours ago," answered Elder Olivia.

"I wonder how Wing Commander Frederick took the news?" Elder Lukas posed the question with a snort.

"I wonder how the entire Wing took the news? After all, a Call of Confidence hasn't occurred for almost thirty solar turns," said Elder Donovan.

"I for one hope it shakes up that wayward commander," snarled Elder Patrick. "Given what we've heard, we had to enact the Call. The Test of True Faith and Test of True Flight will find out if there is any disloyalty to Triumvirate. We'll discover all about this Frederick, that's for certain!"

Cornelius took up the anti-Frederick rant: "Or disloyalty to Krystos, that is who our ultimate leader is, after all. No offense to you, Apostle. Now we'll be able to find out what's in the hearts of the 77th gull-hawks, along with their commander."

"Let's not pre-judge this situation, fellow council members," said Samuel quietly. "The Call will provide the answers. We must remain strictly impartial until then."

"Well, Samuel, of course you encourage fairness in judging, being Elder in charge of the Judiciary," replied Nicholas. "I for one think the evidence we've received surely points to heresy. It's time to find out whose faith is true, and whom are the heretics."

Elder Alexander nodded towards Nicholas in agreement. "I am looking forward to seeing if any gull-hawks crack under the pressure. Surely the crucible of the Call will bring out the best—or the worst, in them. We must cleanse the impure from the body of Krystos, and from Triumvirate!"

"Yes!" "Amen!" "Well said!" Affirmations echoed loudly from half of the Elders, six who seemed be enjoying the moment. A close examination, or better yet an actual, yet confidential poll of the twelve Elders would have re-vealed that indeed six of the twelve High Council Elders had already made their minds up about Frederick's guilt. Three were neutral, with minds locked into impartiality. The final three Elders all had met Frederick, and were pretty sure he was innocent of the accusations, more than likely to pass the Call.

One of those three had a more personal connection with the 77th Wing Commander, had spent time with him, and knew him fairly well. This Elder was quite concerned about the attitude of the High Council, very disappointed in the six with their arrogant prejudice. But more than that was at play here, one more important intrigue, a mystery of the heart. High Council Elder Olivia was not happy about the Call at all, not one bit, and was steaming about the six Elders who so easily judge harshly, and pronounced guilt prematurely, gleefully, without mercy.

For Olivia had fallen in love with the one primarily responsible for the Call—Frederick, Wing Commander of the 77th Wing.

Chapter Two

FREDERICK FOUGHT HARD to calm his shattered self. His troops awaited his reply, his directions, his command! His mind battled a poisonous swirl of emotions: fear, chaos, and despair. What could he do? *Most High, what do I do? Where to from here?*

The gull-hawk lifted his head and looked around. The 77th stood at full attention, in perfect formation, silent, anticipating. Gregory nodded slightly, David flashed a tight smile, and Nathan grimaced a fierce stare. Scanning his Wing, Frederick saw anxiety, fear mixed with concern . . . and longing, pure longing for leadership, and for hope. They were looking to him to lead them, to provide that all important lifeline.

Krystos, what would you do? The gull-hawk was quiet for a moment, when understanding surfaced.

It pulsed inside his mind — *Peace . . . be still . . . and know!* Those wise words, directly from the Sacred Scriptures, rang true to Frederick, and he took a deep, hopeful breath. Commander Frederick turned to the 77th, infused with a small bit of newfound clarity.

"Triumvirate gull-hawks, our Sacred Scripture tells us that in times of crisis, Krystos would seek out a place of quiet and pray to the Most High. It is always true, but now it is especially, poignantly true, we must now follow him even more so. We need to still our minds, calm our fears, and center ourselves on the Most High." Frederick looked slowly around the 77th, spread out over the rocky top of StoneHeart Cliff. "Let's seek guidance in a centering prayer, and seek guidance from Krystos." Once again his gaze swept the Wing—each and every one looked back, waiting, expectant. "As your commander, I will lead you," continued Frederick, "but remember, always remember, that it is Krystos who we follow. If we follow Krystos truthfully, righteously, with all of our heart, our mind, our soul and spirit, then we can succeed—and pass the Call of Confidence." He nodded toward the command team, and then continued.

"For this particular centering prayer, breathe in *follow*, and breathe out *Krystos*. Got it?" Frederick bowed his head and began:

"Follow
    Krystos,
Follow
    Krystos
Follow
    Krystos."

Frederick slowly brought his voice down to a whisper and then went silent . . . but all the time breathing in 'follow,' and breathing out 'Krystos.' Over and over, breathing in and out.

Be my disciple!

The words echoed in Frederick's mind, startling the gull-hawk out of his deep centering prayer.

Where did that thought come from? Frederick kept his eyes shut, and restarted the centering prayer. A few moments later, an answer came. *Of course, follow Krystos, be my disciple, then—become a disciple of Krystos. That's what Krystos said to his disciples: follow me! And what does it take to be a good disciple? Discipline! A successful disciple must have the highest discipline!*

In that instant, Frederick had all he needed. He would take his Wing through Triumvirate basic training, which had as its center the key practice of discipline. It would be rigorous—most demanding—but through this refocused attention to the fundamental Triumvirate lessons Frederick knew he could keep his Wing focused. How could the High Council fail to pass true disciples of Krystos? The 77th would work extra hard and follow an intense schedule, with the reward the chance for a performance which could approach the perfection required.

The Call would happen in seven days, and he must have them ready! In order to pass the Tests, the 77th Wing must attain—and maintain—an advanced level of flying. Although this was possible under normal circumstances, few could sustain it under the Call's excruciating pressure. And yet, he could not panic his gull-hawks—he must take charge, be the calm in the storm, show them he was not afraid, and that they need not be afraid. For fear, a powerful enemy, the mind, soul and spirit killer, could consume them all, as it had consumed—and eventually destroyed—so many gull-hawks before.

"Gull-hawks of the 77th Wing," Frederick began, "You know—and I know—the seriousness of the Call. It is clear to me I am the primary reason we are being Called. Central Triumvirate Command is questioning my abilities and leadership skills. Unfortunately, you are to be tested in the same manner as I; you are caught in the same sticky web that has entangled me. To fail the Call can mean demotion, suspension, and even, in very rare circumstances, excommunication. The Wing being Called typically shares the judgment made about the Commander, but not always. You must not worry about me during the Call; concentrate instead on your flying, your faith, and the Sacred Traditions and Teachings. The Most High and Krystos will never desert you, never, as long as you stay focused, and channel, to the best of your ability, the Sacred Spirit."

"That's enough of a speech. In the upcoming week the 77th will review and rediscover our Triumvirate Basic Training. We will become the ideal disciples of Krystos. The Apostle and Elders will see that we are well versed in the fundamentals of flight, as well as faith. Devoted disciplines, outstanding flyers, and spiritually developed. This Wing will not forget the intense disciple, which forged us as Triumvirate gull-hawks. Do you understand?"

"YES SIR!!!"

All one hundred sixty-one voiced their understanding and approval in one loud, exuberant affirmation. They looked eagerly at their commander, ready to follow his lead. With clear direction given, the Wing's optimism had been restored, and hope replaced their fear.

"Good," replied Frederick stretching his wings in anticipation. "We will resume our daily flying exercises. However, we will close today with what may well be the toughest challenges of the Call, the Sacrifice formation."

Pausing, Frederick looked around, and saw confidence returning to the eyes of the gull-hawks of the 77th. "Squad leaders, get your charges ready—we will return to our level flight exercise." Frederick opened his wings, caught steady ocean wind current, rose quickly above the Cliff, then turned seaward and dropped like a stone towards the beach below. His command team followed just a breath behind their leader as they resumed their precise, time-crafted practice.

The 77th continued throughout the day, giving their utmost effort under the watchful eye of their commander. At the end of the day, the Wing performed the Sacrifice formation, whereby the twelve squads flew in four V's of three rows directly behind the command team:

```
  >      >      >      >
  >       >     >     >       >
  >      >      >      >
```

The Sacrifice formation requires one complete Wing to fly directly into the heart of the enemy, thereby destroying the other's order, creating chaos, and leaving the enemy open to attacks by the other Wings. Unfortunately, the Wing chosen to fly Sacrifice suffers heavy casualties. Still, it was considered a critical—and essential—component to the great cause of defending Triumvirate's realm. Flying with Triumvirate, and the Sacrifice formation in particular had always meant surrendering one's will—and one's life—to the will of the Most High, and Krystos. Surrendering to the Most High meant surrendering to Triumvirate, since Triumvirate was the Most High's "chosen" representative, arbiter and interpreter. To be called to sacrifice for the Most High was the highest glory in all of Triumvirate, for it meant the gull-hawk, or gull-hawks, were emulating in a small way the great and world-transforming sacrifice of Krystos. The Wing performed the formation well, but not flawlessly, so Frederick ordered them to do it again, and again, and again, until they got it right, diving perfectly, precisely, blowing right through the imaginary enemy without thought of their own selves, in true Sacrifice formation.

Afterwards, Frederick gathered the 77th together for the closing prayer and meditation. He spoke one of the traditional Triumvirate benedictions:

"Oh Most High, we give thanks to you for sustaining
    us today,
For challenging us,
And for protecting us.
"You are all, and we are merely feathers, living only
    through your grace.
We pray that You will always bless us,
And that we will always obey your commandments.
"In the name, and through the mighty power of your
    glorious Son . . . .
Amen."

Lapsing into silence, the gull-hawks began the final meditation and quieted their restless minds. When it was over, Frederick gave the order to disperse. Tomorrow was the Day of Rest and Reflection, and it was the 79th's turn to patrol this section of the western coast. The mood, as the Wing broke ranks, was predictably more somber than usual just before the Day of Rest and Reflection, the coming Call pressing like a heavy boulder. Frederick gave final instructions to the command team and the squad leaders before his own flight home. Rising up, he once again caught the strong, steady ocean breeze and let the wind take him toward his place of rest.

Frederick wheeled his way through a low-level cloud cover and soared over a deeply-wooded ridge and into the glacier-carved valley which marked his home. While most gull-hawks lived along bodies of waters in large Gatherings, Frederick lived off by himself just in front of a basalt ridge outcropping which backed up a stand of massive Douglas firs. The stand thrust upward over five hundred feet, giants of the old forest: strong, protecting, and calming with their immensity.

Most gull-hawks feel instinctively drawn into a Gathering, where hundreds, sometimes thousands of gull-hawks live close together—for security as well as social reasons. Frederick and a few others lived a good distance away from the hectic, chaotic nature of Gathering. "So many gull-hawks like ants in a nest, or bees in a hive, packed much too close together," he mused, "with little room for freedom, less time for neighborliness." And yet the small group watched out for each other, and from their respective perches near the top of the firs along with frequent flying kept an eye on the entire valley, well over fifteen miles long.

Frederick dropped below the cloud cover, about a thousand feet above the valley floor, but not far from the tops of the highest trees. Sweeping toward the tall firs, he scanned the usual perch spots for a particular gull-hawk. Frederick felt a burning desire to see his wise old friends. *Well, the next logical place would be the oak grove down by the river.*

With this in mind Frederick readied himself and immediately dove downward.

The gull hawk's speedy descent was witnessed by a solitary gull-hawk settled in a very old, gnarled oak tree, the patriarch of an oak grove which had collectively scoured a living in the valley for centuries, perhaps a millennium. The eldest of the thick, leafy oaks stood proudly on the east bank, while their offspring—numbering in the thousands—marched up a saddleback hillside to its crest.

Frederick skimmed the watercourse's surface at great velocity, banked around a long bend in the river and shot through a narrow cleft, which marked the beginning of the grove. He pulled back hard, then glided to the patriarchal oak. Noticing a spectator, Frederick dropped down to a nearby branch. Frederick said nothing, waiting for the other to speak. He deeply respected Joram, both as a friend, and teacher.

"Greetings, my young friend," spoke the old gull-hawk, his gaze sharp, penetrating, yet exuding warmth and affection. "You look troubled. What's bothering you, Frederick?"

"How do you know something is wrong, Joram? I still don't understand how you're always sensing my emotions. Will you finally, once and for all—today—tell me that you have some kind of psychic power?" Frederick glared at his old friend. "I really want to know—need to know, in fact. Given the challenge I'm facing, I need all the help I can get, including psychic help!"

It was common knowledge among the locals that Joram had been a member of Triumvirate, a warrior gull-hawk of high rank, and, reportedly, had served on the High Council. There were even rumors that he had been in line for the Apostle's Rock, but something occurred which forced his retirement, drove him to live on the edge of Triumvirate, shunned by most.

When asked about his experiences and eventual exile from Triumvirate, Joram revealed little, unwilling to criticize or discuss why he no longer flew within Triumvirate. He did, however, laugh off all rumors of psychic power while freely admitted to emphasizing individual gull-hawk rights over Triumvirate's. He pointed to his stubbornness—combined with an outsized interest in mysticism—as the reason for his parting with Triumvirate.

Their conversation was interrupted as Joram's life-long partner, Dayleen, swept through the sky in a feigned search for her mate. She knew he was probably talking with Frederick, of course. Eventually, she settled on a nearby branch.

"Am I interrupting, Joram? Has something happened, young Frederick?" She cocked her head, her grin infectious.

"You two are quite a pair," replied Frederick, "a couple of over-the-hill mystics. But you are correct, something has happened, something big."

Joram and Dayleen looked back at the young gull-hawk in silence.

Frederick recounted the unexpected visit by the Messenger, the shocking announcement of the Call, and Frederick's suspicion that the Call was aimed primarily at him. Finished, he took a long breath, and exhaled out the accumulated stress.

"Holy Most High . . . The Call of Confidence, who would of guessed? Well, my young friend, everything falls into place, makes perfect sense, in an ironic, cosmic way," replied Joram.

Frederick frowned at Joram. "What in blazes do you mean, 'makes perfect sense?' How can the Call of Confidence make sense? This thing threatens me, my very existence!"

"And Frederick," interjected Dayleen with a quiet voice, "the Call also affords the perfect opportunity to prove yourself, to take the next flight path."

"The next step? Please, you two are speaking in riddles. As usual, of course."

"Frederick, it's been a long day," sighed Joram. "We can talk more tomorrow, after a good night's rest. We've had an exhausting day—nothing compared to you of course—but tiring for us nonetheless. The Day of Rest and Reflection is very timely for someone in your circumstances, and ours too—as your friends. Plan on finding us at the ancient volcano."

Frederick nodded. "Agreed . . . tomorrow it is."

Joram and Dayleen bowed towards Frederick, then jumped off their respective branches and began a slow glide to the river. Catching the wind draft that followed the river inland from the nearby ocean, the two climbed with minimal effort. They found and used the energy from a dissipating thermal to reach the highest tip of the old-growth firs, and disappeared from view. The exiled gull-hawks made their home out on a tiny island just off the coast, a few miles south of StoneHeart Cliff, most western point of the Triumvirate realm.

It was the rare gull-hawk who took the time to get to know Joram and Dayleen, but those who did, such as Frederick, grew quickly captivated by their calm presence, kind hearts and superb flying ability.

While Frederick was one of few who had reached out to the exiled pair, he had taken that risk only in the past year. And despite having spent numerous hours with the two unique, wise, enigmatic gull-hawks, much of the time had been spent in the air. Extremely advanced, high-level, exquisite flying—Frederick reveled in their prowess. Joram and Dayleen shared knowledge—and their friendship— like a glacier, slow, grudgingly. Frederick reciprocated, staying open, but guarded. In the last few months the conversation between them had begun to flow, with trust finally—although still a bit tenuous—established.

He wondered for a moment if nurturing this friendship had been a mistake. *No, that's the least of my worries. Perhaps they'll have some valuable insight for passing the Call. Hopefully!* Frederick sighed and closed his eyes, then shook and stretched his wings wide. He could just see the specks of Joram and Dayleen outlined in the evening sky—his two friends: so serene, so strong, but so unique and . . . strange.

Gathering himself, he dove off the branch of the old oak and flew the short distance to his evening roosting spot. In a somber silence, Frederick watched as the sun dropped from behind a long, flat cloud. The rays cast eerie shadows on the western valley slope while illuminating the eastern ridge line; these wonderful rays touched Frederick at the same time that he landed in the tree top, his day complete.

Olivia fought hard to bury her frayed emotions—it was the only way to survive the hectic, ever-demanding pace of High Council business. As Elder in charge of Flock Communications, she and her staff ensured that all High Council rulings, laws and regulations went out to the various Gatherings and local lay councils. In addition, Olivia managed the multitude of messages which came back to Central Command each day, rated each for importance and priority, and then delivered to the Apostle and appropriate Elder. Olivia and the gull-hawks under her charge sorted the messages into the each of the Elder's respective commands: *Administration,*

Missionary, Communication, Defense of the Flock, Integrity of the Faith, Worship, Judicial, Records, Compassionate Outreach, Reproduction, Daily Needs, and Internal Security. Twelve departments in total, modeled after the twelve disciples of Krystos, all reporting to the Apostle, who represented Krystos, until, of course, the Messiah's prophesied return.

Communications was not the most important department, as the critical ones were typically awarded to the most powerful male gull-hawks: Missionary, Defense, Integrity of the Faith, Judicial and Internal Security. Olivia's membership on the High Council was itself a rarity—only a few female gull-hawks had risen up to serve on the ruling High Council. Since the beginning, in fact, the Council was strictly a male domain—based upon the tradition that Krystos only chose male disciples. Forgotten, of course, was when Krystos flew the sky, females were treated as property of the males, had no significant rights, allowed only to tend to the nest and raise the young. Krystos could not have chosen female gull-hawks to be his public disciples due to the rigid Flock mores of the time. However, the Sacred Traditions did allude to Krystos having several "unofficial" female disciples, but this historical fact had not been openly discussed for centuries.

Only a few generations ago did the reigning Apostle receive a new 'revelation' from the Most High which gave females equal rights, for the most part anyway, and allowed for the most brilliant and/or aggressive to be eligible for Elder of the High Council. Because Olivia knew this history well, she relished her rare spot on the Council, and worked hard each and every day to prove her worthiness—and be an example for all female NorthLand gull-hawks. After all, *her* Messenger gull-hawk carried the bombshell to the 77th Wing about the Call of Confidence. The Messenger was carrying out the orders of the Council based upon the recommendations of the Faith department. Patrick, known as the zealot, was Elder in charge of Faith. It was he who pushed for the Call—based upon clandestine reports from inside the 77th. Despite her own misgivings about Patrick's ruthlessness and her personal feelings toward Frederick, Olivia carried out her duties without hesitation or flaw.

As the time for the evening prayers grew closer, she dismissed her staff with her usual efficient grace, watching in silence as each flew off. As the last flapped out of sight, she began for her own short flight home, but stopped her descent. *I don't want to go home, at least not yet. Maybe a little flying will help my mind, stretch these wings and hopefully burn off some of the stress!*

Olivia flew over her home, a beautiful cove surrounding a small, sandy beach with an abundant tide pool—a privileged assignment due entirely to her High Council rank She could feed right there—which was not only convenient, but pretty much a guaranteed bounty since warrior gull-hawks guarded this ultra-prime feeding ground. Nearly all gull-hawks stayed away out of respect for authority and deference to the privilege of the Council; the only gull-hawks who typically violated the feeding boundary were young male gull-hawks out on a dare!

The image of a daring male gull-hawk brought Olivia a cascade of memories, thoughts that pressed upon her, not to be denied. Frederick, the question of Frederick. *What do I do about him? Honestly, can this ever work? I've thought this through before, how many times? Has anything changed? Well, there's the Call, which adds a new dimension, one more problem. Potentially insurmountable, depending upon the outcome. But that's premature thinking.*

The biggest problem remains—I am of higher rank, with higher status. So difficult with males with a mate who is superior in position, or skill, or rank. It seems to work so much better when the male outranks the female. The Call aside, will Frederick rise to my level, the Council? If not—and the chances of him getting there are slim, how will he react, especially over a long period of time? Could he and I even sit on the High Council at the same time? And what about my feelings, would I respect him, truly, deep down? Or would I look down upon him since his achievements were less than mine? Maybe not consciously, but would I resent him somehow? Olivia shook her head and chuckled. She had had this internal conversation before several times. Well, numerous, many was more like it. The High Council Elder had considered all angles, prayed for hours, rolled the dilemma of Frederick around in her mind over and over. No clear answer had come.

But Olivia was clear on at least one thing. She would not abandon her spirit; deny who she was, or her own journey, and even more, her destiny, unclear as it might be. This conviction broke with Triumvirate mores: first, denial of self, and second, submission of the female ambitions to males, especially her mate's.

Olivia had no problem giving her life for Krystos or to defend Triumvirate. But submission to another just because of gender? No, that went against everything insider her. The Most High had given Olivia tremendous talent combined with a voracious work ethic. Those gifts had to be brought forth in their fullest—and in accordance with the Sacred Scriptures after all.

So while she was falling in love with Frederick, enjoying the newfound feelings, delicious warmth, and powerful surge of joy when she pictured the 77th Wing Commander, she did not want to lose herself in the budding relationship. She would not allow it! Nor would her affection for Frederick supplant her love of Krystos, and her unswerving loyalty towards Triumvirate.

Which brought her back to the beginning, to the same place, the same question. What to do about Frederick? Yes, lately it always came back to the question of Frederick. And there was no answer, at least not now, not yet.

Olivia shook her head and inhaled a long, slow breath, clearing her mind of daring young gull-hawks, like Frederick. She glanced downward at her cove, and signaled one of warrior gull-hawks. After letting him know her plans, Olivia flapped on, anxious to get away, far away from Home Beach, despite the late hour. She crested over a nearby range of dense, forested hills, flowing up and over as they jutted out into the Sound. The High Council Elder pushed higher and higher, exhilarated by the exertion. Looking west, she could see across the Sound and the coastal lands—including a small, snowcapped mountain range—beyond which lay the immense West Ocean. Olivia marveled at this panoramic, stunning view. From her vantage point high in the sky all was quiet, above the cacophony of the Flock.

Here, harmony reigned.

She flew several wide circles, intoxicated by the moment, invigorated by waves of happiness. She could not recall ever feeling this peaceful, this centered, and this joyful—certainly not in recent memory. Holding to that precious feeling, she kept her turning crisp and mind quiet, trying to extend the blissful moment. Too soon, however, concerns intruded and worry grew. How could she feel so happy when the Call was going to bring havoc into Frederick, and perhaps her own life, in just a week's time? A battle of thoughts began, with part of her defending the enjoyment of a few minutes of bliss, the need for such renewal in life's "busy-ness," while another part heaped guilt about the upcoming Call and her part in determining Frederick, and his Wing's fate.

Should Frederick have been Called, Most High? Is he really a heretical mystic, like Patrick claims? No, not Frederick. He seems so clear, with a true spirit, and a strong heart. But if he is a heretic, then he deserves to be exposed and punished. Krystos, what is the truth?

The internal debate went on until a strong wind buffeted her off the circular route; she had to flap strongly in order to maintain her soaring. *Time to go,* she decided, and began a fast descent back to the Flock, her home, her place. *No, not yet!* Olivia wasn't sure where that thought, or feeling, or an urge or something came from, but apparently it was not yet time to head for home. *Where should I go, Krystos?* Scanning the horizon, she spied Community Rock Mountain, an enormous basalt rock rising just off the southern part of Home Beach that provided home to the largest concentration of Northland Flock gull-hawks. Community Rock was always a daunting sight, made more beautiful by the reflected light of the setting sun. Its sheer size and location just on the Sound at the water's edge made its appearance imposing yet majestically attractive.

As Olivia flew closer to the great rock, its attraction grew . . . along with a powerful sense of urgency. Why, she was not sure, for not more than a few minutes ago, she didn't even know that she would come here.

What was going on?

Her heartbeat quickened, and she flew nearer, the din from the many gull-hawks swelling. As she closed in, she felt drawn towards the flying pattern of the gull-hawks circling the great Rock. *Now what?* Brushing aside doubts, but still unsure of her purpose, Olivia instinctively joined the swarm flying around the great Rock: north, east, south, west. It took about a minute to complete the mesmerizing circuit. She glanced down at the Rock as she flew, and saw hundreds upon hundreds of gull-hawks. She hadn't been this close to Community Rock for a long time and had forgotten the mass of gull-hawks that lived there. On the surface it appeared loud and chaotic, but after flying a few circuits around the Rock Olivia detected an underlying subtle order to the chaos.

"Elder Olivia!"

A shout came from just above, to the right side of her. "Look everyone, it's Elder Olivia, flying here with all of us!" Soon she was hemmed in by gull-hawks, flying even closer than before in the circling madness. "Elder Olivia, come join our ledge for the evening prayer!" Several more offers followed, but Olivia focused on the gull-hawk who originally spoke to her, a young male—who looked like a possible Triumvirate recruit—and seemed to have a special charisma, almost like Frederick.

Still circling the Rock, Olivia studied him, and saw in his eyes deep respect, honesty, with a touch of innocence. *I will go with him*, she thought, and immediately a deep calmness washed through her. *This is good.*

In addition to the wonderful sense of peace, Olivia was curious about what actually was happening down amidst that swarm of gull-hawks living on Community

Rock. Olivia realized that she had lived the privileged life too long and wondered if she lost touch with the common gull-hawk. *Perhaps it will help me be a better judge during the Call.*

"Thank you for the invitation. I would be honored to join your ledge. Please—lead on!"

"Yes, Elder Olivia, follow me!" The young gull-hawk careened sharply to his right, barely missing a large contingent of slow flying gull-hawks.

Evening Prayer was mandatory for gull-hawks serving in an official capacity for Triumvirate, but not so for regular gull-hawks of the Flock. Still, it was strongly encouraged and thus followed by nearly all of the Northland Flock, who enjoyed the ritual and accompanying fellowship. The time for Evening Prayer was sunset, now creeping closer and closer. Most of the airborne gull-hawks were busy finding their own homes, their own ledges, and their own nests within Community Rock. The adolescent male landed on a large, protruding ledge, home–or at least a gathering spot—to fifty or more gull-hawks. Several caves opened onto the ledge, which was populated with nests each with its own rocky outcropping that would provide nice shelter in a bad storm. Olivia observed all of this as she flew in and landed next to her escort. He started off, intent on finding the local leader, but Olivia stopped him.

"Wait, I'll walk with you, but first tell me your name, and how you came to recognize me."

"Elder Olivia, I am named Scott Michelson. I will escort you to our local leader, my father. See, he is just over there!" He pointed to an approaching, full grown, powerful looking male. "And many know what the Elders look like, since most of us came to the ceremonies where you, and the other Elders, were sworn into the sacred duty. I will never forget yours, since so few females are chosen for the High Council. You were quite radiant that day, and even though I was very young—it was five years ago after all, I will never, ever forget it, or you. But please, Elder Olivia, my father can more appropriately greet you, and then we can start Evening Prayers. I hope you'll honor us by leading!"

Taken aback, Olivia marveled at the young gull-hawk's words, poise and unabashed admiration. She felt unworthy for such praise, but showed only appreciation in order to not ruin Scott's innocent, naive view of the world, and the High Council. He certainly didn't need to know about Olivia's internal conflict or the weighty matters facing the Council. "Thank you, Scott Michelson. I would be honored to meet your father."

The two walked over to Scott's father, Michael Jacobson, who greeted Olivia with a mixture of surprise and deep respect. The local Elder quickly assembled those gull-hawks present and led them in the sunset service. Olivia was asked to give the closing prayer:

> "Most High, we thank that you have taught us
> . . . how to believe and behave,
> . . . and how to forgive and repent.
> Help us by your Spirit, and the power of Krystos,
> . . . to keep your commandments
> . . . with a pure heart and a clear mind.
> We say this prayer, in faith, trust and truth . . .
>   Amen."

Afterwards, Olivia was invited to bring news of the High Council. They gathered in a large circle, and after

Olivia's turn, she invited each to speak their name and share something about their own life. Smiling with delight throughout, Olivia enjoyed hearing of their day-to-day triumphs and tribulations. Most of all, she valued getting her mind off of her weighty concerns. When the circle was complete and all had spoken, Olivia expressed gratitude to Scott Michelson, Michael Jacobson and the rest for inviting her to be a part of their evening. As she was preparing to depart, Scott spoke once more.

"Father, Olivia should see Great Grandmother Grace. Do you remember that Grandmother mentioned several times this week about expecting a visitor; could Olivia be the one she was referring too?"

"That's right, Scott," said Michael, stopping abruptly. "She told me about a special meeting as well, but if you hadn't mentioned it, I would have forgotten, and we might have missed a superb opportunity!" He grinned towards Olivia, "Elder Olivia, would you indulge us and stay just a little while longer? I would like you to meet Grace, whom we call Great Grandmother, as she is the oldest gull-hawk on Community Rock. She's quite sharp, and has an uncanny, piercing insight into many things. Would you come and meet her? Please?"

Olivia, intrigued by the offer—and with nothing else immediately pressing—quickly consented. She was led to an opening at the back of the main ledge. Several gull-hawks huddled inside, and turned around to face Olivia, Scott and Michael as they entered the cave. On a very large nest of twigs, moss and feathers sat a very old gull-hawk, most certainly the oldest gull-hawk Olivia had ever seen. The ancient gull-hawk watched her carefully, but spoke to the others.

"Please be so kind to give Elder Olivia and me a few moments alone."

Scott, Michael, and the gull-hawks who had been visiting the old gull-hawk did not question or voice any protest. Without a word, they bowed, turned, and left. Although the elderly gull-hawk's request had no impact on them, Olivia felt a strange, growing apprehension. The old gull-hawk's piercing eyes seemed to be looking directly into her soul, seeing through her, knowing her inner thoughts, secrets and fears, no matter how deeply buried. Her mind danced around the possibilities. *Who is this old gull-hawk, Great Grandmother Grace?*

"Who am I?"

The old gull-hawk spoke Olivia's silent question out loud. "It is okay to ask, and it is natural to be curious, even a bit concerned, anxious. Indeed, I am a very old gull-hawk, oldest, although being old isn't really any historical accomplishment, with age can come wisdom. Well, that is if you're willing to learn each and every day, and if you seek it, and are empty enough to receive it—wisdom that is—when it comes. Come, sit with me." She motioned for Olivia to come closer, a warm, welcoming smile on her face.

"For reasons unknown, Elder Olivia, some twist of the Most High's wry sense of humor perhaps, I received a gift, an ability which allows me to see events in the future, and to be given glimpses of the thoughts of other gull-hawks. These glimpses, these visions usually come to me in deep meditation or prayer, my communion time with the Most High. The gull-hawks around me do not know the full extent of my gift, for I only share a small piece of it. They call me "Great Grandmother," although a few, like young Scott and his father, know that I have stronger, uh, abilities. The reason that I keep my gift secret should be obvious. Triumvirate is not real friendly toward mystics, and has, on occasion, excommunicated those who exhibit such talents. Sometimes, although rarely but more frightening—they've executed them!" Grandmother Grace paused, reached out a comforting wing towards the High Council Elder, and sighed.

"Elder Olivia, I have received several impressions lately about Triumvirate, the Council, and you in particular. I was hoping that you would come to me, in order to share with you some very dangerous times ahead." The ancient one stopped, closed her eyes and nodded. Olivia, who had waited patiently out of respect for the old gull-hawk, spoke forcefully in reply.

"You hoped I would come? Forgive my skepticism, but how in Krystos's name could you have possibly known that I would even fly by Community Rock? I never come this way, Grandmother Grace. My being here is a total fluke, a coincidence. And how did you know my name— have you seen me before?"

Grandmother Grace looked at Olivia a long time before replying, long enough that the High Council Elder began to grow nervous. The old gull-hawk took a deep breath.

"Olivia, I know your name because of the impressions—or visions—I've been having, that a female Elder will play a critical role in an upcoming crisis, a crisis already underway. There is only one female High Council Elder—everyone knows about you, even me, a recluse. And your being here a coincidence? Only the Most High knows. You're here, aren't you? I needed to talk to you, and although I can still fly, how can I approach you, talk to you, especially out in the open. Forgive me, but I prayed that the Most High bring you here if, and that "if" is critical, if the Most High felt that you should be made aware of the impressions I've received. Since you are here, and in your own words, you would normally not be, what conclusions would you draw about the Most High's intent?"

Olivia felt her anger rise, her indignation grow.

"Great Grandmother Grace, pardon my frankness, but how can you presume to know the mind of the Most High? What you're saying borders on blasphemy! I came into your cave to pay my respects to you—the community's oldest gull-hawk, and I find something quite unexpected, someone whose words could be considered heretical. Do you really expect me to believe what you are saying?" Olivia looked suspiciously at the old female, whose gaze never wavered, but her ancient eyes revealed a small touch of sadness.

"Please hear me out, and decide in your own time— after serious, quiet reflection and prayer—whether it is true or not. Blasphemous you say? Why do you think I keep my gift hidden? Why is it that Triumvirate believes that the Most High speaks just through the Apostle, or only through Krystos and the original disciples so very long ago? Is the Most High 'of the living' or 'of the dead'?" Grandmother took another deep breath, and exhaled slowly.

"Olivia, the Most High 'lives,' and I use that term loosely since the Most High is eternal, yes? Is the Most High not present right here and right now? Too many think that the Most High is out *there* someplace, but not *here*, now. The truth is, at least for me, that the Most High is not just transcendent, Olivia, but *immanent*, too. Remember, 'within us, between us, in the midst of us?' Such a powerful teaching! It is so unfortunate that Triumvirate chooses to ignore that critical aspect of Krystos's words. The Most High is available all the time, to all of us."

The old gull-hawk paused for a second, and bowed her head, acknowledging the Most High's presence. Olivia could only watch, skeptical of the old one, but nonetheless drawn by her powerful, infectious faith.

Great Grandmother continued: "I did not ask you here to debate theology, orthodoxy or heresy, but to share with you an insight into the present and near future. Let me tell you what I've seen, and please hold your judgment."

Again she paused, and again Olivia kept silent.

"The impressions given to me indicate that our Flock has entered a time of serious crisis, a time when we could see the destruction of Triumvirate. There seem to be two intersecting events. The first involves the Island of Eternal Peace, and a new conflict—of devastating magnitude—taking place around it. The second event begins small but grows in importance, and involves some kind of trial, with a member of Triumvirate being questioned about his faith. You are connected to both events, but you have a very strong tie to the trial, and to the gull-hawk being tried. Later these events intersect, and your role becomes most crucial. No impressions have come to me past a point of decision for you. Perhaps that is where events cannot be foreseen, since choices have yet to be made which today aren't predicable.

"It seems that this trial will cause you great consternation, but after that you will encounter another 'trial', of both a professional and personal nature, where you may have to choose between love and faith, and the Most High and Triumvirate."

Olivia sat, stunned.

She had heard nothing about any current conflicts surrounding the Island of Eternal Peace, although given the
Island's bloody history; a new clash was always possible.
But much, much more perplexing was the ancient gull-
hawk's intimate knowledge about the Call of Confidence.
Only a few in Triumvirate knew about the Call and the
chance of that news, just announced today, leaking to
Community Rock so soon was virtually impossible. And
even more problematic was Great Grandmother's awareness of Olivia's connection to the one being tried, although
technically Frederick was not on trial . . . it was like a trial,
true, but even that small discrepancy did not belie that the
old gull-hawk knew, somehow, some way, about Olivia's
feelings toward Frederick. Despite the High Council's
misgivings, this old one possessed some kind of extrasen-
sory insight that Olivia had not encountered in any of her
travels.

She looked across at Great Grandmother Grace, sitting silent on her nest, patient, with compassion brimming
from her ancient eyes. Olivia's earlier indignation had di-
minished, yet she needed to keep some sense of her own
authority. If Elder Patrick were here, he would claim that
the Evil One was involved, but Olivia could detect no evil,
either in the cave or emanating from the ancient gull-hawk.
Utilizing her training, Olivia began to breathe slowly,
rhythmically, looking inward, concentrating on Krystos.
Great Grandmother matched her rhythm, and a few quiet
minutes passed before Olivia spoke.

"Perhaps my earlier words were spoken prematurely.
You've talked about events and inner feelings known to
only a very few. Triumvirate must always be on guard

for heresy, blasphemy, and self-proclaimed prophets, and we lean toward dismissing any psychic powers as false, or from the Evil One. Sometimes this tendency, this doctrine, squelches wisdom, but most of the time it exposes falsehood.

"In your case, Grandmother Grace, there is real truth in your words, and you may very well have received some kind of inspired or divine communication. Putting aside my skepticism, what shall I do about what you've told me? In your words, the events taking place right now could lead to me to a point where I have to choose between Triumvirate and a gull-hawk who could–although it is a remote chance—end up on trial." `She took a deep breath, and then exhaled slowly. "There is a gull-hawk who matches your impression. His name is Frederick. And even though it would be a tough choice, I would choose Triumvirate, since otherwise would be selfish."

"The impression," said Great Grandmother, "or the vision I received is that your choice will come later, after the two sequences of events intersect. And, understand—there is more to the choice than what you've just expressed."

"What do you mean?" asked the younger female, flustered.

"I wish I could tell you more, Olivia, but I've shared all which has been given to me. The last little bit of impression which I received was that both you and this other gull-hawk—Frederick—might have to give up everything. I'm not sure what that means, but I sensed a feeling of stark emptiness, and then, nothing. There the vision ended."

Olivia stood and began to pace around the cave. "It doesn't sound very encouraging, and there is little insight into what I should do, or change."

"The Most High gives us free will for a very good reason. Just go forward, knowing that you will play a crucial role in a pivotal time for the Flock. Keep focused on the Most High, and Krystos, and the great commandments. You, I— all of us must remember to love the Most High with all our hearts, minds and soul and love each other, and ourselves, as we love Krystos. Keep a clear head, Olivia, for in these times of crisis there will be opportunistic gull-hawks who on the surface appear to be the most faithful, but in the end are seduced by power and could tear everything apart. Know you can return here anytime; for quiet reflection, for conversation, for compassion. I, and this community, will gladly provide you refuge when you need it, whether it is from a physical storm, or a spiritual storm. We'll be here for you."

"Thank you, Great Grandmother Grace. I'll remember that."

Olivia bowed, and her appreciation flowed easily to the ancient gull-hawk, who looked upon Olivia with a loving, complete acceptance that was unlike any she had ever felt. She walked slowly out of the cave and onto the ledge, where Scott Michelson waited. No words were spoken, but an understanding passed between them, that Great Grandmother had touched Olivia deeply, and in some ways, Olivia and he shared a bond. The sun had set, and darkness had risen. Olivia said her goodbyes to the small group of remaining gull-hawks, thanked them, and flew off to her home. There was much to think about, questions to be answered, mysteries to be probed. But not now, as she was exhausted. It had been a long day, an incredible day, and she welcomed her nesting area, and the comfort of sleep.

Frederick readied himself for the quiet of the night, when sleep could give a gull-hawk time to rest, to reflect, to dream, and sometimes to heal. He thought about what had happened to him today. *The Call! Holy Son of the Sacred Spirit. I am in way too deep here, definitely over my head.* Feeling panic begin to edge back in, Frederick began his breathing exercises, the ones taught to give Triumvirate gull-hawks more control in stress situations. The breathing worked, calmed him a bit, and he allowed himself to let go of the Call . . . at least for the night. *I'll lay my anxiety down here and pick it up again tomorrow. Oh, Most High and Krystos, I really need your guidance in the next few days. Your child down here is in big, big trouble, and needs a perfect, Krystos-like performance to survive. Can you lend a hand? Help me to find the error of my ways, and surrender all the more completely . . .*

Frederick's silent petition helped the thoughts racing through his mind to slow, and in their place came a small morsel of composure. Sighing audibly, he recited the standard Triumvirate nightly prayer, which began:

> Thank you, Most High,
> for the gift of the miraculous day."

The graying night sky carried Frederick into sleep. He floated to the tune of a dream, with a strong conscious connection, and deceiving vividness. In the dream he was flying in front of Olivia, who seemed to be pursuing him. He was himself, but he could also sense Olivia's thoughts and feelings. In the dream they were both above the ocean on a bright, sunny day; Frederick was flying a seemingly flawless pattern while Olivia flew close behind, angry at him, concerned yet confrontational.

As she flew after Frederick, he could sense her determination to conquer his free-thinking spirit. Her angry resolve projected easily to him. Frederick felt the dream perspective change, feeling a mixture of rage; love and deep concern flow from Olivia to him. He rode these powerful emotions from her spirit back to where he was flying an amazing pattern with an entirely new wing alignment.

His dream shifted back to Olivia's perspective, and he once again sensed her strong feelings of urgency, her need to control, to change Frederick, rescue him from evil. Frederick became aware of himself, even from Olivia's perspective. In fact, he was now conscious of both gull-hawks simultaneously, and felt an all-inclusive oneness encompass the entire field of vision. Then, he felt his point of reference being pulled upward, not of his own control, but under the power of something far, far greater than his little self. Overwhelmingly humbled, he knew instinctively, without question, that he was in the presence, and under the influence, of the Most High and Krystos. Higher and higher he soared, out of the earth's atmosphere, into the blackness of space itself. Fear overcame him, for he was higher than a gull-hawk could possibly go, and he knew that death was imminent. Crying out, he begged for Krystos to save him. He shouted over and over and over . . .

Chapter Three

HIGH IN THE fir tree, with the predawn quietness and a still dark sky, Frederick opened his eyes, stunned by the force of the dream. The chase, Olivia, and being under the power of the Most High swirled in his consciousness. He didn't want to forget, or lose any of it. No, not this time!

The dream took him back several years, to the time when Frederick first encountered Olivia. They met at a Triumvirate High Council function; Frederick had been invited as a new Wing commander, promoted due to his flying ability and coolness in a series of skirmishes with a small force of Shahadah rebels. One look and he was forever captivated by her presence and her beauty. Their eyes locked and held when introduced, and Frederick felt a powerful surge between them. Frederick bowed first, as was expected for one of lower rank, and the connection was broken . . . for the moment. As one of the guests of honor, his day was filled with official functions, and he found it impossible to speak again with Olivia. But throughout the day Frederick caught glimpses of her, and when he did it appeared that she was also looking out for him, for their eyes met more than once, and each time the chemistry—or whatever it was, continued to spark.

When the time came to depart, Olivia seemed to make an effort to be among those saying good-bye. Protocol would not allow him to display any kind of affectionate gesture, no matter how subtle, given the situation and her

High Council position. But as he started his long flight home, Frederick glanced back and saw Olivia rising up after him. *Most High, do my eyes deceive me?*

Shaking inwardly, he flew a long, slow, banked curve to let her catch up, if indeed she was following him. In just a few moments, she was flying beside him. Frederick suppressed his utter amazement as she glided in parallel, and the two flew together away and out of sight of Triumvirate Central Command and the High Council.

"I hear you're one of our best flyers, Wing Commander Frederick."

"Perhaps." He glanced her way, still scarcely believing that she was right there, flying right next to him. "I'm a good flyer, I think, but just one of many. Triumvirate has plenty of outstanding flyers. And I am always striving to improve, to push my limits, to learn, and become a worthy Triumvirate gull-hawk."

"Well, can you keep up with me? Olivia called out the challenge as she cut Frederick off and flapped quickly away, up above some low-level clouds. The female gull-hawk caught a strong wind gust and rode it higher, while Frederick did his best to match her, using all of his skill and strength. They soared and flew together for a long time that day, over many miles, saying nothing, just flying at the top of their respective abilities. As dusk approached, she led him to a beautiful perch overlooking an alpine lake. They landed on a giant rock, and were quiet for a few moments.

"Well, now I've seen it . . . you are a splendid flyer and deserve your reputation and new rank as Wing Commander—without question. I wished to test you personally, to see whether the confidence I saw in your eyes was carved by experience or just typical male gull-hawk bravado."

"Are we in formal capacity now, Elder Olivia? May I speak freely, without my words getting back to the Council?"

"Of course, Wing Commander. Please call me Olivia for now, and consider our conversation personal, and private.

"Thank you, and call me Frederick." He hesitated a second, measuring his thoughts, considering what he could say, what he could reveal to her. "Olivia, you've got me at a distinct disadvantage. Not only do you outrank me, but also you probably know all about me, given your position as High Council Elder. So let me ask you a question—and forgive my directness—did you fly with me out here *just* to test me? That's not a normal Triumvirate procedure. Why are we here? Not that I mind it, no, I think I'd fly pretty much anywhere if you were next to me."

"Frederick, I like that name . . . *your* name." She paused, looked him squarely in the eyes, joy shining forth. "You are correct; I do have you at a disadvantage. But we are alone here, just two gull-hawks having a good conversation. I've wanted to meet you for some time, ever since I witnessed first hand a few of your exploits at Triumvirate officer training. I had just graduated myself, and had been assigned a job reviewing the curriculum. So few of the candidates show true spirit or any real sign of personality and character, but you had a strong intensity that intrigued me, and a few others in Triumvirate, too. Anyway, after that I lost track of you until your name came to the High Council for promotion to Wing Commander. You see, I had hoped to meet you, get acquainted so to speak, if and when you received your promotion to Wing Commander. And you did it, you earned your own command, and I knew that I would have the perfect chance to see if that drive, that intensity still existed. When we finally met today, I felt a potent flash of spirit, the Sacred Spirit perhaps, along with a special connection between us. I think you sensed it, too."

Frederick stared at Olivia, stunned by her revelation, her candidness. He recovered quickly. "Praise Krystos! I felt the connection, too, although I wondered at the time if it was just my imagination. When our eyes met, it was, if I may speak boldly, as if our souls touched." He stopped, and eyed at Olivia with a wistful look.

Olivia shook her head and chuckled. "Frederick, hold on for a second, you're getting a little ahead of yourself. We do have something, but let's take this new-found, budding flame of affection slowly. It's been said that 'love will find a way.' If we can bring forth something long-term out of this wonderful bond, and if we follow the guidance of the Most High, then is there really anything to worry about?"

Frederick laughed, shaking his head. "You're right! My mind got a bit carried away, zooming forward into the future, imagining all sorts of possibilities. Thanks for the gentle reminder to trust that the Creator's will—will be done, and if that means to bring forth an "us," then so be it." He returned his gaze to her, and looked passionately into her eyes. "Wow! What an incredible day this has been; being honored by Central Command and the High Council was enough, but now meeting you? Olivia, this may have been the best day of my life!"

Olivia approached Frederick, and answered by nuzzling him in a way seen only when paired gulls meet. Finally breaking off, she backed off, smiled broadly, and flapped her wings. "Farewell, Frederick. Our next time together may not be for a while, but I will not forget today. My heart has a glow I've never felt before. It should keep me quite warm during my flight home."

While other recollections had faded, that day remained permanently etched in Frederick's mind. The first touch of souls, the seed of love awakened, and the monumental shift in his life. He basked in the wonderful memory. But the reality of the impending Call jolted him out of his happy remembrance, and his spirit sank. Previously honored for his skill and strength, he now lamented the unfairness of his situation. Neither his Wing Commander position, nor his years of training nor his faith could prevent the surge of anxiety. It felt overwhelming—there was strong, very real possibility that he could lose everything! Sadness, bone-shaking sadness welled up, but he fought against it, struggled to stay composed. *Most High, help me!*

After a bit, Frederick steadied himself—sedate, down, but unbeaten. *I will survive, Most High. With your help, and Krystos, I just might make it through this.* Slowly, determinedly, he gathered his wits, and headed off to meet Joram and Dayleen.

His destination was an ancient, dormant volcano. It was over a year since Frederick had first followed Joram and Dayleen, puzzled as to where the two disappeared to from time to time, and almost always on the Day of Rest and Reflection.

He had been exploring new territory—new to Frederick anyway—and mustered up the courage to check out the volcano, a strange, eerie place that gulls-hawks avoided. Cresting the rim, he had witnessed two gull-hawks on the island in the middle of the lake that filled the lower half of the crater. Although they were many hundreds of feet below the rim, he saw what appeared to be light shimmering around the two. In fact, he thought he witnessed their gull-hawk forms change, becoming less distinct, almost transparent. Not wishing to spy any longer, he circled down to the pair, and the odd light disappeared. When he questioned the old couple about it, they laughed at him, asking if he had been eating fermented fruit, or flying too close to the sun. Although their attitude puzzled him, what surprised Frederick most was that Joram and Dayleen were not angry at his spying; instead, they seemed quite happy to see Frederick, almost as if they were expecting him.

Today, the flight to the volcano seemed so natural, with a light tail wind to make the journey easy, the sun overhead, and, best of all, friends—true friends—to spend time with, and feel accepted. It seemed odd that these two gull-hawks, considered outcasts by most of the Flock, had become his close friends.

As Frederick continued his strong, steady stroking through the early morning air, he stilled the ongoing surge of thoughts and memories, brought his attention to the valley, and his focus on Krystos, Son of the Most High. After all, today was the Day of Rest *and* Reflection, where all gull-hawks should focus on the Creator, the Son, the Sacred Teachings, the Traditions, and above all, the great sacrifice Krystos made.

The volcano loomed ominously in the distance. Even though Frederick knew that his friends were there, and no harm had come to him in any of his visits, there remained something unexplainable about the volcano that made the gull-hawk uneasy. Perhaps it was old tales of volcanoes exploding, perhaps it was what he had witnessed about the old couple the first time he had come here—whatever it was, the volcano remained mysterious, unknowable. This volcano, water-filled at the bottom and with no peak, had stood silent for as long as anyone knew, but who could tell what lay beneath the calm surface of the deep lake? Brushing aside those ruminations, Frederick flew closer. At the top of the volcano's north rim, a remnant of snow clung stubbornly. A tributary feeding his home valley flowed directly from the volcano, receiving much of its life-giving water from each winter's deposit of snow. That same snow—and the seasonal rains—replenished the clear blue lake inside the crater.

The volcano's rim towered above the surrounding forests, forcing the gull-hawk to gain several thousand of feet in elevation, not easy even for a young, strong, highly skilled Triumvirate Wing Commander. Gliding along, he sensed about, looking for ridge lift, or a thermal, anything to give him the needed boost upward. Worry crept in as no lift came initially, but he stroked forward, hoping, and was rewarded with a sudden, strong upsurge.

Thank you, the Most High! His gratitude flowed naturally as he crested the rim and banked immediately to right, intent on circling the rim. Glancing inside the crater, Frederick spotted Joram flying just under rim, with Dayleen circling several hundred feet below. Joram signaled for Frederick to follow, and wheeled into a tight bank around the massive rim. The two males caught up with Dayleen and their circles grew smaller and smaller as they approached their usual hangout, the island thrusting above the ancient lake. After landing, Dayleen spoke the opening prayer:

"The kingdom of the Most High does not come by observation

It cannot be said that it is over here,
Or over there.
For behold, the Kingdom of the Most High
Is within us, through us,
Between us, surrounding us,
And transcending us."

The three concentrated on the flow of breath in and out, becoming one with the rhythm, one with the Most High. While fighting to quiet his mind, a question nagged at Frederick. Although he respected the old couple, he didn't feel that he really *knew* them. They were mysterious, like the ancient volcano.

Triumvirate teaching was full of forebodings about those claiming to know the Creator, the Most High. And there was the exile, of course. Still, Frederick knew that the prayer spoken by Dayleen lay within the official Teachings, just not emphasized. He asked:

"Why did you begin with that particular prayer?"

"I love it," responded Dayleen, returning Frederick's intense gaze, but tempered with a warm smile. "Even though Triumvirate does not use this prayer very often, Krystos spoke it when asked when 'the Kingdom' would arrive. He was trying to tell us that the Kingdom—of the Most High—is not a specific time or a place, but a state of being, a . . . level of consciousness. The Most High is immanent—here now, and at all times, eternal but present in each moment. And the Kingdom is energized when two or more of us come together in communal, loving spirit." Dayleen nodded toward Frederick, exuding the warmth of her spirit, and continued.

"Did you know Frederick, some ancient teachers who lived long ago, before Triumvirate, taught that the gull-hawk soul was a part of the Most High, that each of us is connected to the All-Encompassing Great Spirit, which we call the Creator, or Most High. And one of Krystos's own followers declared that whoever loved Creation *knew* the Most High, and that when we *love,* then the Most High dwelled—you know lived, or resided—within us! It's a powerful teaching, and a reminder of another way which we can bridge the apparent gap which exists between ourselves and the Most High, a gap with is paradoxically real—and illusionary—at the same time."

"I don't think I've ever heard something like that articulated so clearly, so true. It mirrors my own, deepest convictions." Frederick looked at Dayleen and shook his head. "But I also have beliefs, thoughts which aren't quite as firm, inner doubts, questions. Uncertainty—even a small sliver—does me no good with the Call fast approaching. We're all pretty good flyers in the 77th, so that's not an issue. But," and here Frederick looked around, and lowered his voice to a confidential whisper, "I'm not convinced that salvation comes exclusively through Krystos. I wish I could believe like everyone else, with no qualms or reservation towards Triumvirate's Sacred Teachings." A deep shudder shook Frederick. *Do I tell them?*

"You've alluded to these doubts before, my friend, but have held back. That's understandable, in this world ruled by Triumvirate where it's not safe to express doubt. What's said here stays here, period. But it's your life, your choice."

Frederick took a deep, slow breath. "I had an experience, one that I have not spoken about before—not to anyone." The young gull-hawk closed his eyes, measuring his response. "What happened to me planted these doubts about Triumvirate doctrine." He looked at his friends, reluctant to share his long-held secret. Joram and Dayleen returned his gaze with their usual warmth and loving kindness, quiet, patient. *If I can't tell them, then whom can I tell? And when?* Frederick paused again, shaking his head.

"A number of years ago I witnessed members of the Shahadah Flock, gull hawks who believed just as strongly as I did, but in a different way. Their faith had been passed down over many generations, sacred teachings from El-Rah—their name for the Most High, and with miracles performed by some of their saintly gull-hawks and prophets. The Shahadah sacred teachings, faith, devotion, works and love were righteous, honest, beautiful—and pierced my own wall of distrust and unbelief. Furthermore, they possessed a special regard for Krystos, although they see him differently than us." Frederick looked intently from Joram, to Dayleen, then back to Joram.

"So no one else in Triumvirate knows about your experience?" asked Joram. "Interesting, although not entirely surprising. What exactly held you back?"

"Fear," replied Frederick quickly. "You two are open enough to hear me, but I've still kept it buried. However, others of the Flock—well, I'm quite sure I'd be tainted, maybe even shunned, if they knew what happened."

"Would you tell us now, Frederick?" asked Dayleen, her eyes shining bright, love underpinning her words.

"You have us really curious," interjected Joram, his smile wide, "and we'll never stop asking about it. Plus, it will feel good to share, to release this . . . this burden."

Frederick nodded. "I was stationed on the southeastern border; and through an odd turn of events, or some strange workings of the Sacred Spirit, I rescued a Shahadah gull-hawk. You see, after flying for miles with some fellow Triumvirate gull-hawks on a training mission, we were engulfed by a blinding storm. I became separated from my group; after several hours of aimless flight, I came across a gull-hawk—obviously wounded—being chased by a half dozen black eagle-hawks. Without thinking, I dove at them, driven to help this 'brother' gull-hawk. I knocked a couple of them out and wheeled quickly away with those remaining in fierce pursuit. Krystos was with me, or something, as I eluded them and then, somehow, found my way back to this fellow gull-hawk, now hiding in a tree, quite shaken up and with a wing tattered from their attack. He would have died there, but between my knowledge of Triumvirate healing techniques and his guidance, after a couple of days the two of us limped to his family's home. Apparently, I had crossed the Great Straight that divides Triumvirate and Shahadah and was in their territory!

"My eyes were opened in the first few hours of my visit. Malibakr and his Shahadah family believed as fervently in their own teachings as we do in the Son and Triumvirate teachings. But despite my Triumvirate faith, they offered me splendid hospitality, most grateful that I had saved Malibakr—who they had given up for dead.

"The first thing I learned was they don't worship Moham—the founder of their faith—like we worship Krystos, but regard Moham as the "Prophet of the Most High." And second, while they don't believe that Krystos is the messiah and savior of the world, they pay Krystos deep respect, calling him the "Spirit of the Most High." Those two things surprised me. It was also interesting that Malibakr's family were cousins of the Shahadah ruling clan. They were proud and boisterous, but humble and devoted at the same time.

"Despite my being Triumvirate—their sworn enemy, they treated me like a son. It was most amazing! I really liked Malibakr, and will never forget his sincerity, honesty, and discipline. We became close in our short time together. We also exchanged flying techniques . . . each eager to impart something of our own to the other. And he could fly, well; they were all outstanding in the air. Supremely-controlled recklessness or tightly-harnessed wild-wind are inadequate descriptions of his and his vast, extended family's style of flight. It was plain to see why they give us so much trouble in battle!" Frederick grinned wryly at his friends, remembering the encounter, and his realization of the Shahadah prowess.

"Their devotion to El-Rah—their name for the Most High—was also quite impressive: A minimum of five times a day they stop what they are doing—completely stop—and pray to the Most High—while always facing in the direction of the Island of Eternal Peace. The strength of their faith puts many of us to shame.

"I was asked a ton of questions about Triumvirate life and beliefs, and I tried my best to answer—sharing the teachings of the Son and the Most High. And they reciprocated, passing onto me the teachings of the Shahadah faith, like their daily prayer. After a couple of weeks, his family flew me in the direction the nearest Triumvirate outpost."

Frederick took a deep breath, his unburdening complete, and waited for his friends' reaction.

"There is something special about you, Frederick. When we first met, I could see it in your eyes, and now I know some of what makes that specialness. But you kept those events well hidden, even from us." said Joram.

"Your experience with Malibakr's family was a gift from the Most High, in some respects, but now it seems like a curse, creating the inner doubt," added Dayleen.

"Now, well, it really bothers me! While I don't regret that experience—I treasure the memory, actually—it means I can't believe like everyone else. I follow Krystos with all my heart, all my strength, my entire mind and spirit. I just don't know if that is enough, if my devotion will be enough"

"Maybe you're the one with the correct beliefs, maybe a little uncertainty is good," suggested Dayleen. "Uncertainty allows an opening for growth, learning, wisdom."

"That's great in the long flight, but in the short flight, right now, I have this massive test upcoming, you know, the Call of Confidence?"

Dayleen nodded. "Frederick, my guidance is to focus on Krystos. Neither Joram nor I have any doubts about Krystos—his virtuous life, impeccable teachings, unmatched flying, and mighty sacrifice. He showed us the Way, he lived the Way, he was the Way. Arguably the most authentic gull-hawk to ever fly the skies of this planet. We follow him."

The 77th Commander drew in, then exhaled a long flow breath. "Wow, Dayleen, that was beautifully said. It parallels my thoughts, my own conclusions. But my doubts—and I have several—aren't that Krystos was 'the Way.' No, the biggest, most dangerous doubt is that I don't think that Krystos is the 'only Way.' You know, fundamental Triumvirate doctrine, sacred teaching number one. After being with Malibakr's family, I believe—or more like

I'm *convinced* they are living a true 'way' as well. How am I going to pass the Call if I cannot even get past the first sacred tenet of our faith?"

"That's a dilemma, no question about it, Frederick," said Joram. "You might get lucky, and be able to provide the answer you just gave, that you follow Krystos without question, believe in him with no doubts. That may be enough."

"So that's one major concern," interjected Dayleen. "What else is bothering you?"

"I don't know," replied Frederick quickly. "Well, I do know, or at least have a pretty good sense of my disagreements with the Triumvirate creed. I take to heart the admonishment by one of the Ancients to 'know thyself,' after all." He fell silent, shifting his gaze from Dayleen to Joram and then past them, to the massive inner wall-like northwest rim of the dormant volcano. *We are so small compared to this volcano, just momentary specks of dust compared to its age and size.* He looked back at his friends. *Do I trust them at an even deeper level, reveal even more about myself and my doubts of Triumvirate?* Frederick shook his head, and exhaled another deep breath.

"We're your friends, Frederick, but we haven't know each other all that long. Share only what you want, what you are comfortable with," said Dayleen.

"Personally, I'd love to know, as I am very curious," said Joram with a smile. "Dayleen is the one who has better social graces, while I just probe till the bitter end."

Frederick took a deep breath. "You can imagine I'm pretty guarded about these kind of thoughts—Triumvirate has ways of finding out all kinds of things. After all, they must know some of what I am thinking because I am being Called. Or suspect what I *might* be thinking . . .

"But here goes, my second major disagreement with our Sacred Scriptures is their portrayal of a huge, insurmountable gulf between the Creator and us, the created. Except Krystos, of course. He is fully divine and fully gull-hawk, simultaneously, it is taught. But that leaves the rest of us on the outs, so to speak, and that concept, or reality, seems incorrect to me. Wrong, a fundamental error."

"I kind of agree with you, Frederick," said Joram. "Actually, I agree a lot with you."

"Me too," added Dayleen, her tone serious, as she rolled her eyes at Joram. "That particular teaching always seemed like a misperception of our true nature and misunderstanding of what Krystos taught. It's one thing to point out that each of us feels, at times, cut off from the Most High, separated. That is an accurate observation and assessment of our condition. But Triumvirate's solution to this problem is, in my opinion, inadequate and arguably mistaken."

"Exactly!" Frederick jumped up, flapping his wings. "I think that Krystos was telling us that we—like him—are sons and daughters of the Most High. 'Our Father,' he said. *Our!*"

"Yes, and he asked each of us to *follow* him," interjected Joram. "How can we do that if we are so different than him? We'd have no real chance. "

"So what's the next big problem?" asked Dayleen.

"Original sin really bugs me."

Joram and Dayleen exchanged knowing glances, nodding simultaneously. But it was Joram who asked the obvious question.

"What bugs you about original sin, Frederick?"

The 77th Wing Commander shook his head. "Everything! And it connects to the wide gulf issue, too.

The basic concept—that we were created in some original perfection, then apparently disobeyed the Most High in a questionable story that seems to really limit the Creator. This act by the innocent, naive first two gull-hawks initiates the wide gulf between gull-hawk and the Most High. Or does it? That question is not asked or answered in the Sacred Scripture. Anyway, flash forward, and enter Krystos, who, depending upon which Sacred Scripture you read, must die to bridge the gulf, pay the blood price for all gull-hawks, reconcile us back to the Most High. Well, if we accept him as savior, it does. I don't know for sure, but to me, it sounds like a convoluted, twisted tale, made to fit someone's guilty conscience and political agenda, and has since the first time I heard it. There is so much of this story, this concept, that does not make sense to me."

Joram looked at his friend, silent for a moment, a grim smile frozen on his face. When he spoke, his tone was measured, almost stern. Frederick wondered if he had revealed too much. The jovial, humorous Joram had given way to determined seriousness.

"My friend, I think you've encapsulated legitimate, significant questions about Triumvirate doctrine. Neither Dayleen nor I are fans of those teachings, and in fact share your concerns. That's part of the reason that we are sitting here talking to you, living in this quasi-exile, instead of sitting, for example, on the High Council back at Home Beach. Your doubt is reasonable, logical. You've identified weaknesses, perhaps even errors in the Sacred Scripture.

"But Frederick, at this moment, right now, focusing on those questions is not helpful for passing the upcoming Tests. They're valid questions, and Dayleen and I would love to explore them in depth with you later. Say, after you succeed?"

"You are in a tough spot," added Dayleen. "These questions, these doubts can, and most likely will, surface during the Call. But others have doubts, too, Frederick. You are not alone. Remember that these doctrines began as ideas, ways of explaining the current state of affairs. For example, why do we fell cut off, separate? A great query! Insightful gull-hawks back then came up with answers, explanations as to how we got to where we were. The answers pointed toward the truth, but they were not the truth in totality. But over time those explanations became doctrine, sacred teachings, and we forgot that they were really just descriptions, speculations, ways of better understanding ourselves and the planet we live in. We gull-hawks desire certainty in this world — that quest for certainty is a strong impulse in a world and universe so much larger than us, so full of mystery, dangerous, and one in which we all will die, and are aware of that dreadful fact." She paused, and looked intently into Frederick's eyes.

"The key to passing the Call is to focus one hundred percent on Krystos. Forget all the myths, the religion about Krystos, explanations that seem inaccurate, doctrine that originally pointed the way but over time evolved into immutable truth. You have a divine spark, and you have Krystos. That should be enough."

Frederick nodded, no words forthcoming. He had unburdened himself, shared his deepest fears. He looked at his two friends, friends who seemed closer now. They did not reject him, not one bit. It felt good, as good as the warm breeze which ruffled his feathers and brought him the smell of the island pines and birch. He took a deep breath, marveling in that earthly, delicious smell. Joram, however, was looking upward, eyeing the sky, and raising his wings.

"Speaking of Krystos, let's see if we can't follow Krystos more nearly with a little flying!" exclaimed Joram. The old gull-hawk gathered himself for several long moments, stretching his wings, twisting his neck back and forth. After bowing his head, Joram looked to the sky and sprang upward with a series of powerful wing strokes, a pause, then more strokes, a pause, and multiple strokes again as he gained several hundred feet of altitude in a few short seconds. Frederick and Dayleen watched Joram rise above the volcano floor using this unorthodox style.

Without warning, Joram veered backward in a tight loop, then plunged straight down towards the island. Frederick grew nervous as his friend quickly reached the pull-out point, then passed it!

The young gull-hawk threw a worried glance at Dayleen, but she calmly watched her mate mere seconds from death. Turning his gaze back on Joram, the young gull-hawk spied Joram twisting his torso sideways while fanning his wings in a peculiar shape. Joram banked to his left and just before crashing into the hard earth, he shimmered while simultaneously shifting his wings into the horizontal flight configuration, and shot across the lake's choppy surface. As the volcano wall came rushing up, Joram wheeled to his right. Curving sharply, Joram sped towards Dayleen and Frederick, then braked hard and dropped in front of them with two barely perceptible flaps.

"Where in Krystos's name did you learn that ridiculously dangerous pullout?" Frederick gaped at his friend, stunned.

"I've had a few outstanding instructors, my young friend," replied a heavy breathing Joram, "and they drilled me without mercy. You see, I was a slow learner, but fortunately my teachers were unrelenting."

"You could fly like that, too," suggested Dayleen.

"Really?" asked Frederick. "You think so?"

"No question, Frederick," replied Joram, "if—and it's a big if—you'll work extremely hard, push yourself beyond your limits, channel your inner Krystos."

"I'm game," nodded Frederick, "maybe after the Call?"

"Yes." Joram smiled at Frederick, and after a sidelong glance toward Dayleen, took off again.

Throughout the rest of the day, the three frolicked in the summer warmth, alternating between Triumvirate elementary, intermediate, and advanced flying techniques. In between, the old couple shared words of encouragement and well-placed teachings, all centered on Krystos. As the sun set they soared high above the volcano and the adjacent river valley, catching the ocean-fed wind currents and a few straggling thermals to heights where breathing was difficult, and gull-hawks rarely venture.

When all color had faded, they began the journey to their respective homes. Joram and Dayleen peeled off to their small island. Frederick followed, not yet wanting to part with his friends and their precious companionship. The three found a great, rocky outcropping, and sat silent, reveling in the wonder of the night sky.

Frederick broke the stillness: "I really appreciate all that you have done for me today—I feel spiritually nourished! But before I go, do either of you have some final advice—or guidance—for someone facing such an intimidating challenge as the Call of Confidence?"

"Are you that someone?" asked Joram.

"You're a real funny gull-hawk, Joram," retorted Frederick.

"Answer Frederick's question, Joram," said Dayleen sternly. "This is no time for joking!"

"Just be in the moment, Frederick, what else can you do? You fly as well as anyone, and you know what Krystos taught, and you do your best to follow him."

Dayleen came over to Frederick and gave him a hug. "All you can do is fly with Spirit in the first Test, and to answer with your truest heart and clearest mind throughout the second Test. That way, when you are finished, you'll have done your absolute best, and no regrets."

There was nothing more to say, no more advice to be given, so they said their good-byes. Frederick flew homeward, tired yet glowing with the after effects from the Day of Rest and Reflection. His mind tumbled with the day's thoughts, ideas, and the new flying ways. Although physically exhausted, Frederick could not sleep, so he filled the space of the dark night praying for an answer to his looming obstacle. Finally, he surrendered to the Most High, giving up, letting go, and it was then that he found not a final answer, but blessed relief in the bosom of sleep.

Chapter Four

FREDERICK BREAKFASTED EARLY to avoid contact with others—this was no time for small talk. He needed to prepare for today's exercises, and distractions would do him no good. Although the 77th Wing Commander wanted to pass the Call, more important than his own needs were those of the gull-hawks under his leadership. He could not—he must not fail them!

Winging his way to StoneHeart Cliff's exercise area, Frederick felt the warm glow of courage building, resolve emerging. He whispered a quick prayer of thanks to the Most High, grateful for this resurrected strength. A dense fog bank reached up several hundred feet from the beach, blanketing the surrounding area, broken only by the cliff and surrounding hills. It looked like rocky islands amidst a calm, immense lake of white. He was the first to arrive at the 77th's ledge, a place familiar and friendly after two years of command.

Off on the horizon flew a squad of gull-hawks on patrol, which according to the schedule, would be that of the 79th Wing. On the Day of Rest and Reflection, the 77th, 78th, and 79th Wings split patrol duty along this section of NorthLand's west coast. Frederick shook his wings, and thrust upward for a quick flight before his gull-hawks' arrival. He turned towards the cool ocean breeze and dropped down into the cloudbank. Flying blind in the thick fog, the wing commander swooped down, his senses amplified, alert for the Cliff, the ocean, or gull-hawks. He could actually *hear* the water's distance, could smell its salty closeness, and pulled into level flight a mere ten feet from the top of the choppy, white-capped waves. Reveling in bliss, Frederick drank the exultation from this spirit-guided, joy-filled flight. Approaching the southern edge of the fog bank, he found another strong breeze blowing against the cliff, steady, cool—the salt smell full, invigorating. Frederick shaped his wings to take advantage of the deflected airflow, followed the wind toward shore and rode the ridge lift up the right side of the Cliff. Rising above the cloudbank, the gull-hawk swooped to his left and once again approached his Wing's ledge.

This time he was not alone, 77th gull-hawks were massing in anticipation of the day's exercises. When the entire wing had gathered he led them through the proscribed first prayer and meditation. Afterwards, he yelled out his first command of the morning:

"Squad leaders, inspect your gull-hawks! Sound off when you are ready for high-altitude flying." Frederick watched the squad captains hustle to assemble their charges.

"Squad three ready!!!"

"Squad twelve ready!!"

"Squad seven ready!!"

After all twelve squads had checked in, Frederick began—his voice stern, his posture strong and erect: "Gull-hawks of the 77th Wing, we will rendezvous at the height where we can see SkyToucher on the eastern horizon, two miles up. There, we will fly Victory formation straight down.

"Yes, many of you are thinking, it is a dangerous maneuver with the addition of the fog. But, you have done it before and know instinctively what to do. And truly, all that is different today is that your vision will be obscured at the end. Triumvirate gull-hawks of the 77th, here is a splendid opportunity to use that inner vision we talk about within our faith but so rarely *actualize*." He paused for a second, looked around at the assembled gull-hawks and almost choked up, overwhelmed by the moment, and the presence of one hundred sixty-one gull-hawks, focused on his every word, all unified towards one goal. He shook his wings, flapping them in a gull-hawk show of dominance, and continued, "Panic and adrenaline must be controlled; use the prayers of protection and guidance during the flight downward. It is up to me to pull us out of the downward plunge in time; I will be guided by the Sacred Spirit. You've seen me fly—I will not fail you! Do you trust your training? Do you trust yourself? Do trust me? All right then, can *you* do it?"

There was only a momentary pause, before the crescendo of one hundred sixty-one gull-hawks all cried out in unison, "Yeesss Siiirrrr!!"

"Good." Frederick's face and voice reflected his determination and faith. "Now focus within."

The gull-hawks remained in the silence, undisturbed by the steady breeze or the slowly dissipating fog, gathering the courage required for the test their commander had placed in front of them. After several long moments of silence, Frederick raised his head, and called out:

"Gull-hawks of the 77th, let's FLY!!"

One by one, the squads rose into the crisp morning air. A strong wind now buffeted the high cliff and the gull-hawks struggled to keep their squad in a precise **V** behind their respective leaders. Using instincts crafted over millions of years and honed by years of intense instruction, the twelve squads and command team remained in formation without collision or falter. With dogged determination the 77th rose upward; from a distance, the Wing appeared as a giant corkscrew, turning perpetually counterclockwise in the relentless climb skyward. Although the thermal weakened as the gull-hawks ascended, powerful wing strokes maintained their momentum and there was no perceptible change in speed on their flight higher.

Reaching the proper altitude, Frederick pulled out of the spiral with a flick of his wings, the Cliff a miniature rock far, far below. He veered right and signaled to Gregory to bring the command team into horizontal mode, to be followed by the squads. Satisfied, Frederick then began a wide circling pattern which each squad mimicked as they reached the proper altitude.

When the last squad had joined the circle, Frederick wheeled about and swept through the upper atmosphere in a dizzying series of turns, loops and rolls designed to test his gull-hawks' ability to fly without flaw and follow without failure. Only an occasional squad leader squawking at their charges—demanding perfection, expecting excellence, disturbed the high altitude. A wing brought 1/8 inch closer to the body, the beak dropped a tad, a tail or wing feather barely misadjusted up or down, each was a minute change needed to ensure the internal integrity of the formation and, ultimately, enhance their survivability in battle—or now—succeed in the great, fearsome Call.

After many minutes of this controlled, demanding flying, and satisfied with the Wing's performance, Frederick signaled for the Victory formation. The squad leaders joined up in seconds, as they had been anticipating this, the coup de grace. Frederick made one more circle, glancing back to see how the Wing maintained the victory pattern. The commander mouthed a quick prayer for protection of the Wing on their descent down, took one more look back at the twelve squads and received indication from the leaders that all was ready. Gregory and Frederick's eyes met, and in an unspoken agreement, Frederick altered his wings and plummeted toward the ocean below.

No matter how many times he plunged into a gravity well, Frederick experienced fear. Swallowing hard, the gull-hawk forced the fright out, unwilling to yield to this paralyzing force. He accelerated at a blinding pace, knowing all to well that at this speed—if he moved his feathers the wrong way by a fraction the increase in air pressure would tear him apart. Frederick shook off the fear boiling just below the surface of his focused consciousness. As the gray fog bank loomed closer and closer, Frederick hoped his gull-hawks were remaining poised in this rush towards the sea. He fought the urge to glance back–that movement would kill him—and kept his attention squarely on the approaching fog. The gull-hawk reached terminal acceleration and relaxed a fraction—he could go no faster. Frederick gauged the distance to the fog, estimated the additional space between the fog and the sea, calculated the time required to enter the fog bank and then the pull up in order to avoid crashing into the water. *Five, four, three, two, one—using* the countdown brought the Wing Commander's mind and body into a single focused point as he prepared for the treacherous pull out.

Frederick knifed into the blanket of gray, adjusted his feathers, and at two hundred miles per hour curved perfectly into a level flight pattern, zooming through the 'ground cloud,' cutting a parallel to the Cliff. He altered his wings again, applying a braking shape. Visibility in the fog was only about a few hundred feet, but he could still see the ocean laying in wait a mere twenty feet below. He was able to look back at this speed, having slowed to a glide, and saw his command team right behind, and the remaining squads—all twelve—lining up crisply, still in Victory formation. He led the Wing in this horizontal flight pattern for several minutes, enjoying the claustrophobic nature of the fog ceiling. Then, with a barely perceptible signal to Gregory, Frederick banked hard left, towards StoneHeart Cliff. At first invisible, the Cliff suddenly sprang into full view. Crossing onto the land, Frederick led the way back to the 77th's large wind-hewn ledge.

Settling down in his usual spot, he waited until all of the gull-hawks had landed and lavished praise on them for their performance. They were giddy with the accomplishment, the release of fear and adrenaline rush. Frederick allowed the Wing to congratulate one another before leading them through a short prayer and time of silence. It was critical to shift their mood and get them ready for the next lesson.

"You are aware that the Test includes challenges to our flying, our faith, and our learning," began the Wing Commander, using his best voice, a mixture of command, and compassion. "This week we will review from the beginning the Teaching of the Flock, from the time before Krystos through the formation of Triumvirate. Most of this will be a review, but it is essential that Triumvirate history be on the front of your brain and subject to immediate recall, without hesitation, and most important, without doubt. Hold your questions until we break into squads. At that time your squad leader will lead an open forum on our topic; the command team will be joining the squads randomly to observe and answer the most serious queries."

Frederick cast a long look around the Wing; all were in rapt attention, lining the rocky ledge, crowded together so they could more easily hear their commander. It was an awesome display! "Long, long ago, many generations before Krystos, the Most High chose to reveal Himself to this Flock. Not trapped in nature—and in need of constant appeasement—as were most of the gods of that day, the Most High both created *and* commanded nature, meted out justice with loving kindness and tender mercies, but whose jealous, vindictive and wrathful nature occasionally resulted in the death of many neighboring non-Flock gull-hawks."

He paused for effect, glanced at Gregory, who silently urged him on, took a deep breath, and continued, "Our ancestors—the Ancient Flock—saw then, and Triumvirate sees today the Most High as the supreme creator of the universe, who gave gull-hawks dominion over the air, and pronounced Creation as *good*. But the first pair of gull-hawks' turned away from their Creator, and brought misfortune and suffering into the world.

"Still, despite our 'gull-hawkish' tendency to fall short, miss the mark, or sin, our Flock before Krystos—which we call the Ancient Flock—strove mightily to improve our meager lot, live in accordance with the Most High's commandments, while all the time giving total and complete credit to the Creator. Despite a life span a mere blink of time compared to the infinite age of the Most High, we're truly children of the Creator, required to make judgments, given the ability to create, and unfortunately, to disobey, and to destroy. We are free to choose.

"The Most High gave the Ancient, pre-Son Flock five basic commandments to guide them, which Krystos expanded to twelve:

"Worship only the Most High; do not worship material things;

Do not call upon the Most High without true need."

A gust of wind buffeted across the large 77th ledge, momentarily knocking Frederick off balance. He grinned, and heard laughter from several in the Wing. "There you go, a clear sign that not I, but the Most High is indeed in charge." Frederick finished the twelve commandments, and then returned back to the history of the pre-Son Flock.

"Recall that the Ancient Flock traditions were steeped deeply in teachings, sayings and warnings from gull-hawks known today as the Old Prophets. They shared an unwavering conviction that each gull-hawk, since he or she is a child of the Most High, had rights that even Flock rulers could not violate. Risking disfavor from rulers and the Flock, and perhaps their very lives, they spoke out against inequity, moral transgressions, and any behavior that had displeased—in their view—the Most High. And, they foretold the coming of many events, including the coming of Krystos, the Messiah, and only begotten Son of the Most High.

"From this history and lore did Krystos arise." Frederick finished abruptly and grew still, letting the lesson be absorbed by the gull-hawks, giving time for the thoughts to be processed and allowing questions to be formed. After a few seconds, he spoke again: "Squad leaders, gather for instructions; all others—at ease. We'll reassemble in five minutes."

With the twelve squad leaders gathered around along with the command team, Frederick imparted his instructions to them.

"The basic lesson outline for this week is to discuss the Ancient Flock, the life of the Son, the formation of the Triumvirate, and the history of the Triumvirate up through current times. On Friday we will review the most critical elements of our doctrine. If you have trouble with a question, signal to me and I'll see if I can help. Emphasize that although questions are tolerated here, none will be tolerated during the Call. I want to remind you that the Call is not only about your faith, but also about your loyalty and submission to the Triumvirate. Here in the 77th I allow for individual interpretation of the scriptures within broad guidelines, but the High Council will demand strict, orthodox recitation of Sacred scripture. Put personal feelings, thoughts and beliefs aside, my fellow gull-hawks. It is time to honor the original teachings of Triumvirate, to go back to the basics—Krystos's life and great sacrifice, and the creeds and beliefs which were birthed back then. Start with a prayer, proceed immediately into discussion, and make sure you get everyone to participate! Understood?"

A few questions came up from the squad leaders, were answered, and the twelve flapped over to their respective squads, formed circles, and began, while Frederick and the command team remained. Gregory looked at Frederick with a mixture of bemusement and respect.

"What's that look supposed to mean?" Frederick asked, a challenging tone in his voice, not sure what to expect.

"The new Frederick, orthodox, tougher, hard-line, a real straight-laced Triumvirate gull-hawk," replied Gregory, accepting the challenge with a deft counter stroke.

"Thanks a lot, First Officer. You know this is one monster gale storm challenge in front of us—and now is no time for my typical unorthodox approach, joking, quasi-mysticism, or questioning authority. I don't like it any better than you, but what's the alternative?" Frederick replied with an exasperated shrug. "These gull-hawks depend upon me."

"With the Wing Commander's permission, may I disagree with your conclusion?" Frederick nodded his ascent to Gregory, who continued, "While I agree some adjustments should be made this week in order to prepare for the Call, why completely change the routine, the banter, the camaraderie, all the wonderful fellowship that has made this Wing one of the finest in the Triumvirate? Don't we want to keep tensions at minimum in order to wring the finest performance out of the 77th? I submit, Commander, that the gull-hawks need your warmth and compassion as much as they need your strength and discipline. They follow you with ferocity because of your well-roundedness, the combination of superb flying, courage, intelligence, wit, deep compassion, and mystical insight. Alter the focus a tad, turn the intensity up a bit, of course, but stay loose. You're too tight, Frederick! I can't remember where I heard it, but it seems that there are some sacred teachings that say 'a gull-hawk reaches the ultimate Truth by working without anxiety about results, without desire, with the heart fixed on the Most High.'"

Frederick smiled at Gregory, and breathed a sigh of relief. He put his wings over his eyes, and shook his head with a small chuckle. "Well said, my friend. And thanks so much for making your point with a possible heretical teaching during the week of the Call, where no other

Teachings are remotely accepted. Unfortunately–or fortunately—it applies, and you're right in the rest of what you
say."

Frederick stopped a deep breath. He looked intently at
Gregory, and lowered his voice. "Help me to balance seriousness with laughter. You have my permission to inject
humor into any situation that desperately calls out for it. But
Gregory, we've got to stay focused, the Call can ruin a gull-
hawk's life–our lives—if any significant mistake is made.

"I'll also be a steady reminder for you to stay loose,
keep your sense of humor." A wide smile broke across
Gregory during his reply, his eyes glowing with deep respect and affection towards Frederick.

"I need you to do that. Now, has the First Officer finished with his instructions to the Commander?" Frederick
inwardly gave thanks for Gregory's insight and frank
nature. He was such a treasure; no doubt the best first officer in Triumvirate. Outwardly, he showered praise on
Gregory, putting voice to his thoughts, "Truly, no commander has been blessed with a finer first officer. I will be
sad to lose you, my friend—you are ready for your own
command." Frederick blinked back a tear of gratefulness,
which did not go unnoticed by Gregory, who beamed
and nodded a silent thank you. Without further words,
they joined one of the squads in mid-discussion about the
Island of Eternal Peace.

"Commander Frederick, do you think Triumvirate
will ever drive Shahadah off the Island of Eternal Peace?"
The question came from Jason, a senior member of the 6th
squad.

"Yes, I do think Triumvirate will someday drive
Shahadah off the Island of Eternal Peace." He looked

around at the squad; all eyes were focused on his words. "And years later Shahadah will no doubt drive us off the Island, and then after that we'll defeat them, followed maybe by a peace treaty, then war again, and on and on. It is a source of perpetual, back-and-forth conflict. I don't see it ever ending, without divine intervention from the Most High, that is."

Frederick turned toward his first officer. "Gregory, how about you? Have any additional insights for Jason and the squad?"

Gregory looked at Frederick, a bit taken aback. "Well, I agree with you, Commander, but I'd like to bring the focus to today. Both of our Flocks consider our traditions to be the one chosen by the Most High, and neither wishes to yield even a winglet. Of course I believe ours is most righteous, but the Shahadah believe just as strongly about their faith. Both Flocks consider the Island of Eternal Peace holy, sacred ground and have been willing to sacrifice the blood of many in order to possess it. I don't like sharing the Island, but the current 50-50 arrangement beats the never-ending killing when we are at war. Honestly, I don't see why we can't just get along, live and let live."

Frederick listened intently, focused on Gregory's words, and the sound of his first officer's voice. At the end of Gregory's answer, Frederick's eyes closed suddenly, and involuntarily. An intense white light burst within his mind! The light filled him, and then narrowed down into a point of incredible, sun-like brilliance. An unexpected tranquility descended upon him, pervaded his body. Frederick somehow knew that the illuminating point of white light was the source of the gentle yet all-encompassing enveloping peace. Simultaneously, Frederick felt unconditional love emanating from the light point and blend with the outpouring tranquility. *Most High? Krystos?* Overwhelmed with awe, the gull-hawk could do no more than stay focused on the light, and wait. After a few seconds, Frederick sensed new, alien thoughts welling from within:

"Appearances in the near future will be seductively deceiving. Keep a clear mind and true heart at all times. Seek out the two old gull-hawks; learn from them, and receive their friendship. Keep flying the Way and the devastation to your Flock can be reduced, although much blood will flow regardless."

Frederick was paralyzed, captivated, but the whisper in his mind continued, *"The Most High speaks through gull-hawks in the all the flocks, not just in ancient times but also in the present. The truth is revealed to each in the way that they can receive it, and no one flock has the exclusive answer to salvation or enlightenment. Frederick, you will be a messenger between the flocks. Someone must be willing to examine and understand the similarities and differences of Shahadah and Triumvirate. Keep your faith centered in My light, and know, dear Frederick, that you are my beloved child . . . as are all my children!"*

With that last utterance, the trance-like vision that enshrouded Frederick faded—he was left with conflicting feelings of dreadful importance, overpowering puzzlement, and shock. As those emotions echoed through Frederick, a new, frightening trepidation surged as he opened his eyes and remembered where he was—in a discussion group with one of his squads and his first officer, Gregory! They stared at him with amazement, concern, and just a hint of fear. Seizing control, Frederick called immediately for Nathan, the Wing's senior healer to join him along with Theresa, the 9th's squad healer gull-hawk. He apologized to the squad leader, gave Gregory temporary command, and placed himself under the observation of Nathan. Gregory ordered the other squads, who had become aware of the strange happenings in their midst, to resume their discussions. Frederick, Nathan and Theresa flew off one of the many niches in the Cliff, and when they were alone Frederick addressed his senior healer.

"Nathan, examine me and determine if I am fit for command. I seem to have had some kind of fainting episode back there. Perhaps that drop from the sky affected me more than I anticipated. Theresa, please observe."

The Wing's senior healer inspected the Commander carefully, not sure of what he was looking for but following orders nonetheless. Standing not far from where Frederick was in the squad circle, Nathan had become aware that his commander had fallen into some kind of trance state. This was by itself not completely unusual—in fact, he had seen Frederick in trances before on a few occasions, and was extremely curious if any physiological after-effect would be noticeable. He examined Frederick's eyes, listened to his heartbeat, breathing and pulse, looked over his wings, put him through some short walking and flying exercises, and asked a series of questions. No signs of abnormality, no evidence of physical change, all mental facilities operational and functioning at high ability. The elusive trance—mystical or not—did not linger very long, if at all. Inwardly, he swore a minor oath, since he had been hoping to discover something, anything, to further his understanding of Frederick's apparent malady, or if it was indeed some kind of extraordinary or mystical power. Nathan swallowed his feelings, faced his Commander, and gave the diagnosis:

"I can find nothing wrong, Commander Frederick; the examination yielded no problems whatsoever. I pronounce you fit to return to duty. Excuse my bluntness, Commander, but what exactly happened to you? Can you describe it?" Nathan narrowed his eyes and looked directly into Frederick's eyes, intent upon an answer. Theresa glanced between them, an invisible observer in this examination and inquiry.

The 77th leader thought for a few seconds, choking down a wave of anxiety before it revealed itself on his face. Frederick dared not disclose the details of what happened—he would be excommunicated for sure! Still, he could not lie to Nathan, who was completely loyal to him, but he could not tell the whole truth since Theresa, a fairly recent addition to the Wing, Frederick was unsure about . . . he had a funny feeling about her. No, he could not completely trust Theresa, but having two healers clear him would be better.

"I felt very lightheaded." Frederick shook himself all around. "In fact I saw white light. After, I may have blacked out for a few seconds, but the next thing I can clearly remember is regaining consciousness and seeing everyone looking at me like I was a ghost! Thank you for the thorough examination, Nathan—you've shown your mettle once again. Theresa, unless you have anything to add, I'm ready to rejoin the Wing." He looked steadily at both of them, with confidence and command. Theresa, although silent and just a bit intimidated, watched closely. She had observed him go into the trance, or whatever it was. Could he have been possessed? Possible, but there was no real, tangible evidence. How could she report on these occurrences if she had no proof, nothing tangible to grab onto?

"No, Commander," said Theresa after a moment of hesitation "I don't know what to say . . . I don't have any experience with blackouts like you described." She looked down, unwilling to face the gull-hawk she was spying on. She deflected away from that line of thought, and said to Frederick, "Commander, I hope you don't have a relapse anytime soon, especially with the Call nearly upon us. We need you!" He acknowledged her strong statement with a brief nod, turned and thanked Nathan, and then moved quickly back toward his command team and the squads. This was all done without hesitation, as he preferred to avoid any further questions, and more importantly any repeat of the trance. *What did happen, Most High?* But this was not the time for questions or doubts. Maybe later, when he was alone, or with Joram and Dayleen.

The remainder of the day proceeded without any additional psychic phenomena or other unusual events. The Teaching Time was followed by several grueling hours of flying exercises: banking, soaring, gliding, loops, stalls, level flight, and landings. These were not that difficult when flown under normal circumstances, like a gull-hawk just out on a morning stretch, but staying in precise formation within a squad of twelve gull-hawks, multiplied by twelve squads, now that was truly difficult! There was no room for error, none.

Worship followed flying, with each of the squad leaders leading their respective gull-hawks in prayer, meditation, prayer, and song. Frederick relished the singing time, knowing that song can not only uplift the sorrowful heart and focus the wandering mind, but it could also bring delightful sound to the day and, more importantly, help harmonize and unify the Wing. Afterwards, a grateful Frederick spoke the benediction:

"We give our utmost thanks, Most High, for the
    many blessings you have provided us today.
Our ability to fly, to speak, to learn, to listen, and
    to sing are wonderful gifts given abundantly
    according to Your grace.
We ask that you sustain us, support us, and guide us
    throughout this crucial week, as we prepare for
    the Call.
We ask as well for your love and forgiveness for our
    many sins since we are only dust without Your
    unwavering love and illuminating truth.
We say this prayer in the perfect name, and through
    the impeccable power of Your almighty Son, our
    glorious savior and Lord, Krystos Gull-hawk."

The lessons continued throughout the week, each day filled with flying formations and exercises, lectures about the history of Triumvirate, discussions with the gull-hawks of the 77th, silence, prayer and song, and as the week's end approached, tensions had escalated. A mixture of foreboding fear and exhilarating anticipation permeated the Wing, challenging Frederick's command and presence, confidence and patience. No more mystical events occurred, thankfully, and before anyone could imagine the week came to an abrupt close—the intense training, teaching, practice and prayer concluded. As the last day began, the 77th was keyed up, nerves frayed and adrenaline pulsing. During the closing lecture, about mid-afternoon, a squad of gull-hawks approached from the south, along the shoreline. Frederick recognized a High Council's protectorate escort, and his pulse quickened with dread and anticipation. *Now who's this?* His mind flashed to Olivia. *No, she wouldn't come.* The Wing Commander took several deep breaths, searching for a semblance of peace. *Why am I getting so worked up? This Elder is not Olivia, so relax—calm down.* Internally he felt fear, but his outward demeanor projected a stoic image, his body stiff, at attention, waiting.

As the gull-hawks drew near, Frederick was able to get a better look at the Elder flying in the midst of the protectorate squad. The gull-hawk's heart stopped. It couldn't be, but it was—his fantasy, and worst nightmare, all in one.

Olivia!

A new dose of anxiety surged, and his pulse quickened. Shaking off the apprehension, he called out an order for his gull-hawks to assemble for inspection; they responded immediately, the week's training showing in the gull-hawks' crisp movements. The protectorate circled the 77th's ledge twice, scanning the surroundings with practiced, hard eyes, ensuring the safety of the High Council Elder. They landed with a minimum of flap, and walked in unison the few feet to where the Wing Commander stood. Frederick followed protocol by bowing, thus avoiding Olivia's eyes, and uttered a greeting, quashing his angst as best he could:

"Elder Olivia, welcome to the 77th's home ledge. To what do we owe such an honor?"

"Greetings, Wing Commander Frederick," replied Olivia, speaking convincingly as High Council Elder, with no trace of the feelings that they had shared. "And greetings to the 77th Wing." She paused, looked around, impressed by the Wing's attentiveness. "I have come at the request of the Apostle, the High Council, and Central Triumvirate Command to wish the 77th well, lead your Wing in prayer, shed light on the upcoming proceedings, and ensure that everyone understands exactly what lies ahead."

All one hundred sixty-two gull-hawks stood still as stones, riveted by her words. Olivia surveyed Frederick's Wing, inwardly proud of their discipline, dignity and respect. As she looked around, she nodded here and there, acknowledging them. Then, she flapped her wings, and began, "Please, be at ease gull-hawks of the 77th, but do listen closely." At her command, the breaths of one hundred sixty-two gull-hawks exhaled simultaneously, countless wings shook, bodies shifted, and a few quiet squawks were heard.

Olivia waited for the Wing to settle down. "As usual, after first light tomorrow morning you'll assemble here." She began and then in great detail, Olivia explained the Call. She spoke long and clearly, ending with the words: "If you pass, as we hope, your Triumvirate status will be as before, and in fact will be enhanced because you'll have proven yourself under the most intense pressure. But if you fail, you may be asked to leave Triumvirate. That judgment, however, is reserved until later." Her eyes caught Frederick's, then swept around the Wing, once again making eye contact with as many as she could, touching them as only someone with the gift of charisma can. "I have heard," she said, "that the 77th is among our best flying Wings, that you follow the mission of Triumvirate with great zeal and love; that you know the Sacred Scripture and the Teachings well. My wish is for the 77th to live up to your reputation, to let your true selves shine through, and that you pass the Call of Confidence. Please bow your heads and join with me as we ask the Most High for a sacred blessing in the challenges to come."

Olivia led the Wing in prayer, then spent the next hour meeting quietly with each squad. The command team's turn was last—when their eyes finally met, Frederick saw something flicker ever so briefly across Olivia's face before she turned toward the command team and led them in a short prayer. She and her protectorate stood off to the side as Frederick dismissed the Wing with instructions for tomorrow morning's assembly:

"Gull-hawks, do what you must this evening to prepare for the journey and upcoming Test: sleep, meditate, pray, spend time with loved ones, fly, or whatever you are guided to do by the Most High. Be here at sunrise tomorrow, ready for flight. With Krystos's help, we can—and will—succeed." He turned toward Olivia, and said, "And thank you very much, Elder Olivia, for coming all of this way, for sharing your blessing, and your prayers with us. We are truly grateful." He bowed to her, she bowed back, and the Wing began to disperse, their last evening of freedom beckoning them away, to their nests, perches and loved ones.

Frederick asked the command team, who were always the last to leave, to come before sunrise for meditation and preparation. He glanced at Gregory, waving him away, so only he and Olivia remained, along with her protectorate squad. Olivia instructed her squad leader to wait on the 77th's ledge. She walked to Frederick, and they flew a short distance to a rocky outcropping at the very western point of StoneHeart Cliff, out of earshot of the squad. The wind buffeted them, pulsing strong and weak, almost like the waves crashing into the beach far below. Frederick turned toward the ocean, momentarily transfixed by the sun descending toward the horizon. Olivia gazed first at the ocean, then at Frederick. He felt her stare burning into him, and he turned to her, unsure of what to do. She looked sadly into his eyes, a mixture of compassion and pity shining through.

"Frederick, I'm sorry you have to go through this. How are you holding up?"

He looked down for a moment, still puzzled as to what to say, what to feel. Gathering himself, he said, "With the Call almost upon us, I am feeling okay, Olivia, not great, not terrible. Anxious, sure—nervous, of course, but my focus has been good. The Wing is performing better than ever, reciting their lessons with near perfection, and showing a remarkable amount of faith in the Most High, and in my leadership. I believe the High Council is really testing me and my influence over the Wing. But what is not clear is why you have come here today, out of all of the Elders. Not that I mind! I love seeing you, Olivia."

Olivia laughed, shaking her wings and her head back and forth. "Frederick, are you blind? While we've had almost no opportunity for any kind of connection, my feelings for you have remained alive and true! I wanted to come and send you off with not only my official presence but also, more importantly, my personal blessing. I am not one of the judges for the Call, and you should be aware that no contact is allowed with any other gull-hawks for those undergoing the two Tests. So this was my chance to see you, and I volunteered to deliver the Council's message." She looked deeply into his eyes, her affection unmistakable. "I miss you, Frederick, and I'm hoping that after the

Call–assuming you pass–we can have time together, to see where the spark we share takes us."

Frederick stood quiet, stunned by Olivia's confession, her open admission of—what was it? Caught up in the warmth, Frederick sighed, hung his head, and looked directly into Olivia's eyes. In that instant strong feelings flowed between the two gull-hawks, their souls touching, a silent expression of love echoing wordlessly from one to the other.

Frederick asked: "When the Call is completed, do you really believe we can start a relationship—that our duties will allow the time—the occasion?"

"I don't know the answer to that, Frederick. We'll pray in earnest and trust in the Most High to guide us." Olivia paused and exhaled a deep breath. "I wish I could stay longer, but protocol demands that I return to Home Beach. May Krystos's blessings fill you during the coming Call! We will be together soon, Most High willing."

Olivia and Frederick said good-bye as a Wing Commander and an Elder should. Each fought the potent force which threatened to unite them in a passionate embrace, a lovers' kiss, to merge into one. This was just not the place, and both knew it. Frederick turned away and lifted off. Circling over Olivia, he whispered an oath of love, and after watching her take flight, began his short way home.

The rush of seeing Olivia quickly faded, however, and he flew back empty, just a touch sad. The marvelous reds, pinks, oranges, and purples of the mighty sunset could not shake the gnawing concern about the Call. Aware of his negative thinking, Frederick angrily shut off his pessimistic thoughts as he raced homeward, but even a clear mind did not erase his anxiety. *What am I really afraid of? It's no secret to me-how will I answer the questions of the Test of True Faith portion of the Call?* It was that thought that troubled him so, and caused the gull-hawk to descend into melancholy once again. Forgotten was the mystical union with the Most High, the reservoir of faith developed over many years, the outstanding readiness of the 77th, and the unexpected expression of love from Olivia. All that remained was a solitary gull-hawk against the graying sky, uncertain and alone.

Chapter Five

DAYLEEN WOKE JORAM early the next morning, before dawn. Joram eyed her groggily. "It's . . . it's dark. Why are you bothering me?"

"Hurry, honey," replied Dayleen, ignoring her mate's cranky protest. Let's see Frederick before he takes off. I'd like one last time with him before he heads to the Call."

"Wonderful, Dayleen. Okay, okay, I'm up. You should have been a drill sergeant." He saluted with a flourish. "Please, my lovely bride, after you."

Dayleen brushed the playful sarcasm aside and took off, flapping away from their home ledge. It was only a few miles from their offshore island to Frederick's valley, and after some firm persuasion by Dayleen, the sleepy Frederick joined his two friends in morning mediation, one which extended beyond traditional limit as the gull-hawks wanted to hold the tranquility, and delay Frederick's departure. Finally, Frederick broke the quiet moment.

"It's so nice of you two to come. I had a tough, awful night. I kept thinking about the Call. I can't lie—I am afraid of what might happen—what they'll do to me if I can't pass their tests."

Joram and Dayleen waited, feeling the anguish in their friend. There was nothing they could do. The 77th commander recounted the previous week, including the trance-like encounter with the Most High, and Olivia's surprising send-off. His emotion broke through, frustration winning out:

"Why me? What have I done that the Most High would put me through this crap? It doesn't seem fair. I'm mad, I'm afraid, ticked off, anxious."

Again the two remained silent, knowing that Frederick had to answer his own questions. They both fought the urge to speak as they watched their friend agonize.

"Join in any time, you two. I'm not fond of one-sided conversations." When the two looked mutely back, Frederick continued: "Are you trying to tell me something? You're usually happy to add commentary and opinion. What—do you want me to come up with my own answers here?" He glared at them, frustrated at their continued silence. "Well, I don't have any answers. None! I feel like I'm caught up in a massive storm, with no control, no power, no choices left. And you two sit there like a couple of bumps on a log. C'mon, help me!!"

Joram began, then Dayleen, each sharing soft words of comfort, soothing suggestions and assurances. Slowly, gently, they brought the anxious Triumvirate gull-hawk warrior back to his deepest self, and highest truth, Krystos.

Frederick regarded his friends, grateful for their presence. "Thanks so much . . . that definitely helped. If I think too much, it's overwhelming, but at least I've got a kernel of sacred truth that maybe—just maybe I can hold onto, no matter what comes. And speaking about what's to come, Joram the psychic, do you have any foretelling of the future?"

"Only the Most High knows for sure what lies ahead," replied Joram gingerly, sidestepping Frederick's probe. Now was not the time to reveal the vision that he and

Dayleen had glimpsed about Frederick's future. "I'm convinced, my young friend, that there is something about you which is unique, singular and special. Have you forgotten about the inner whispers—don't those experiences tell you something? Do you think that Spirit speaks so clearly to everyone?"

"And when you feel that anxiety returning," interjected Dayleen, "remember the sacred tradition, *be still and know that I am the Most High.*"

Too soon it was time for Frederick to leave. He said goodbye to his wise, loving friends, choking back sorrow as he flapped away. Glancing backwards, he saw the two gull-hawks flying below him in circles, perfect circles. He sighed, felt a deep sense of strength surge unexpectedly within, and simultaneously heard a small voice whisper to him.

Let go!

Frederick froze momentarily, which caused an immediate altitude loss. He quickly regained his composure and asked in a challenging voice, "What did you say?"

There was no reply, only silence. Frederick flew on, still in shock over the intrusion, and the seemingly foreign voice whispering in his mind. *Let go!* The two words echoed in his mind as he flapped steadily toward the Cliff, eager now to meet the 77th, but not so eager to make the dreaded flight to the place of reckoning. The Call of Confidence— the words made Frederick shiver.

Frederick was one of the last of command team to arrive, and they looked worried, especially Gregory. Talking with Dayleen and Joram had caused him to be a few minutes late, and Frederick berated himself for taking those moments with his friends. *My first—and last—concern has to be the 77th, what was I thinking?* And yet, the brief time with the old gull-hawks had helped him, had revived Frederick from his depression, and perhaps he could pass on some of that renewed spirit to his charges.

"Commander," began Gregory, "the Wing is awaiting your leadership." Gregory's eyes sparked with indignation, his tone noticeably impatient. Frederick's guilt grew over his tardiness, and he squelched any idea of sharing his early morning experience. He guided the command team through a short prayer and mediation, and talked about the upcoming flight to Home Beach while the rest of the Wing arrived. The 77th performed the rituals as a whole while awaiting the impending arrival of the escort from Central Command, due any minute. Frederick shook off the tension and focused on the cool breeze and tangy salt smell of the ocean.

Revived somewhat, he moved the Wing into a few basic exercises, leading the Wing around off the Cliff and down the long beach to the south in tight, precise formation. A less-than-impeccable formation would make a bad first impression on the escort. Frederick had drilled the Wing of the importance of initial impressions. Although Frederick hated the importance that one's image carried within the Flock, he had learned that this concern was part of the Flock's reality—a reality which was sometimes ugly and shallow and pompous. Nonetheless, he had instructed the 77th again and again how a solid first impression could positively influence those who would judge the Wing during of the Call.

Frederick led them higher, and soon spied five specks in the distance.

Here they come!

The escort team approached, flew in a wide circle around the Wing, and began the flight back to Central Command and the High Council of Triumvirate. No words were needed as Frederick and the Wing followed compliantly. A large escort was not needed for the one hundred sixty-two gull-hawk Wing, since disobeying the Call meant instant excommunication. Gull-hawk behavior was ruled in part by the fear of excommunication, the eternal banishment of the soul, with the banished gull-hawk becoming invisible to all in the Flock. Even though the Son of the Most High's recorded words were silent about excommunication, Triumvirate had made it an integral part of the Flock's belief system. If the glory of Heaven wasn't enough of a tasty meal to shape a gull-hawk's potential behavior, the fear of eternal banishment usually got a gull-hawk back in true flight—with 'true' flight being defined by Triumvirate, of course.

Frederick pondered excommunication and the Son of the Most High as they flew steadily forward through the early morning light. The burden of his thoughts prevented him from seeing the beautiful valley below him, a lazy river meandering through a vast grassland and the snow-capped mountains off to the southeast. *I doubt Krystos would even think of excommunicating me for the teaching which I shared or the odd events which have happened to me. He could see my heart and tell that I have no malice towards him or the Most High. I wish the High Council was as insightful and loving as the Son, that there was someone to talk to about what has happened to me, the mystical occurrences and the Most High-like voice.*

Suddenly Olivia flashed into his mind, and his heart leapt, then sank.

Olivia could have been—should have been the one to talk with him and really help out, but now, with his life and career in question, the gull-hawk wondered if she would even talk to him again if he—heaven forbid—failed the Call. *No, Olivia is an Elder of the High Council after all. She'll need to keep her distance. Even if I pass the Call I still may be tainted by it. Despite what she said yesterday her position may prevent further contact, at least any contact of real substance. If I pass the Call, I'm told all will be forgiven and forgotten, but gull-hawks don't forget, and too many never forgive. I've seen that way too often—negative stigma remains—suspicion is not wiped away. No, there's no salvation in Olivia, and quite possibly no future.* The gull flapped on, a dark cloud of negative emotion surrounding him on this otherwise cloudless day.

Frederick wasn't the only one with intense thoughts. Gregory was still stewing from Frederick's inexcusable lateness. *What was he thinking? He should have been the first one there, preparing the space, being the leader that I know he can be. But maybe he isn't such a great leader, maybe this Call is justified, and maybe we'll fail because of him. Well, I shouldn't be surprised—the teachings do say not to put your faith in gull-hawks, only in Krystos, and the Most High.* Gregory felt a touch better, although still somewhat guilty since he had put his faith in Frederick and thus had violated the Teachings. *I hope they don't ask me about that in the Call.*

The Wing flew on, each gull-hawk lost in his or her thoughts, feeling nervous yet exhilarated, fearful yet hopeful. The wait was over; the journey, however dreaded, had begun. After the overland flight, they had reached the western shore of a great body of water called Triumvirate Sound, which stretched from the north of StoneHeart Cliff many miles to the east before turning east and south as it penetrated the interior of Triumvirate territory. Onward they flapped, past the white capped mountains, the lush green islands and peninsulas, the light brown beaches and the wind-eroded cliffs. Along the way Frederick noticed a few other Wings going through morning exercises, and he felt a pang of regret and a longing for the sweet routine of Triumvirate practice. Maybe he could repent, admit to his transgressions (whatever they might be), accept admonishment, and return to his command and the Cliff patrol. This sense of relief washed through him and he indulged deeper into the feeling of forgiveness and a return to normalcy. A small sense of hope bubbled up inside, and a smile came to his beak. He glanced backwards at Gregory, and gave him an encouraging nod. Gregory looked at his commander with a puzzled face, wondering what Frederick was thinking about—what had brought forth that smile? Frederick saw the puzzled look, and was about to speak when the escort called out a warning cry—danger!

Frederick squawked for the Wing to tighten into a defensive formation and scanned the sky for the danger. There it was! Off to their right flew a dozen large, powerful birds—by their wing strokes and light-colored heads Frederick guessed the twelve to be rare white-headed giant Blackhawks.

Over the generations gull-hawks had eliminated most of the other species of birds, removing them as competition and proving gull-hawk superiority and status as the Most High's *chosen*. The rarely seen Blackhawks, almost twice the size of the gull-hawk, had successfully resisted and were now revered by both Triumvirate and Shahadah as special, almost sacred. Their white heads, pure black bodies and white wingtips provided a visual reminder to gull-hawks of the dual nature this world: black and white, night and day, good and evil. Gull-hawks avoided the oversized black birds at all costs, afraid both physically and spiritually of these large flyers.

Frederick gauged the distance and Blackhawks' speed and trajectory; they would cross directly in front of the escort and the Wing! He trembled, wondering why the Most High had sent such a powerful sign. He felt the Wing's concern growing and the formation becoming ragged. Frederick squawked loudly, redirecting their attention from the giant birds to him. "Stay in formation!" he cried, "Focus on Krystos!"

The escort slowed to ensure the Blackhawks' clear passage. The attending warrior gulls kept a protective formation around the Messenger, bracing for a possible fight. Even with their intense warrior training, the giant birds' presence was affecting these elite gull-hawks, and they felt a rare feeling, deep fear. The Blackhawks glided swiftly in front of the Wing, glanced at the gull-hawks, and the one in front cried out a fierce warning.

Will they attack an entire Wing?

Frederick posed the question while calculating the odds. It usually took a squad—thirteen gull-hawks—to ensure defeat of just one these massive creatures. *We should prevail . . . Most High willing.* Still, an attack like this, out in the open in a chance encounter . . . or was it chance? Frederick had never heard of the reclusive Blackhawks attacking unprovoked such a large force. Defend, yes, but attack, no. *What will they do?*

The twelve passed by, the warning cries continuing, and now from all of them! Frederick got his closest view ever of these magnificent birds, their huge wingspans, large, completely white heads, and muscular, sharp talons tucked under their black, powerfully feathered body. *So who exactly is the chosen ones of the Most High? We've done well, sure, but those Blackhawks are something else entirely. How do they fit, exactly, into the Most High's plan? They probably know nothing of Krystos, so are they damned? Or are they exempt? I don't honestly know!* But the unique creatures banked slightly to change course and in a few minutes, they appeared as dots on the east horizon. It took awhile, but eventually the Wing and escort settled down to complete their journey, the Blackhawks' interruption mostly forgotten.

The gull-hawks turned westward, crossed through a small mountain range covered by a thick, lush forest. They reached the northern edge of the Triumvirate Sound in the evening and rested in the cliffs high above the water. After eating and bathing in the mouth of a river the next morning, they resumed their flight, Home Beach the goal. Trepidation increased as they neared the place where each had been initiated into the Triumvirate. Filled with fear and foreboding, the beauty of this part of the flight escaped the 77th. Frederick spied Home Beach off in the distance. There were a myriad of Wings performing training exercises on all sides of the Beach, and several flying a wider perimeter, on patrol no doubt. He wondered how many knew about the Call, and felt ashamed, suddenly exposed to the judgment—shallow and uninformed it might be—of so many gull-hawks.

The Messenger and his escort vectored around and away from Home Beach. Frederick surmised that the High Council would not allow the Wing the privilege of flying over Triumvirate's sacred beach, and certainly would be prevented from landing on Home Beach. *At least not now, while my Wing's very soul and integrity is being questioned.* No, the Wing was brought to a lesser beach around Sun Point to the west and south of Home Beach. Frederick glanced about, looking for any gull-hawks that he might know, but hoping in his heart that none would recognize him—or his Wing! Even though Frederick felt innocent of any major wrongdoing, the stigma of being Called was a clear negative. A glimmer of hope existed, however. They had been told that a Wing which passed the Call was often honored since to pass meant the gull-hawks of the Wing were not only superior flyers but also possessed a deep, committed faith, two essential ingredients to success in the Triumvirate. *At least that's what they said; I hope it is true!*

One gull-hawk which Frederick did desire to see, one gull-hawk who he believed to be his main, and perhaps only ally outside the 77th, was Olivia! He surreptitiously scanned the sky, while still following the Messenger, his heart pounding in a mixture of fear and hope. Where would she be? Unfortunately, time was not his friend; the Messenger circled a small, deserted beach and began to descend. Frederick had no choice but to follow, leading his Wing to their apparent resting place for the evening, and place of waiting for the Call to begin. *No Olivia, at least not yet.*

The Wing landed in perfect formation and stood in silence, awaiting orders from the Messenger. Frederick had prepared his gulls-hawks on protocol here; although he didn't know exactly what was proper in this situation, he had instructed the 77th to behave according to the strict Triumvirate code of conduct for all enlistees—speak only when spoken to, follow orders explicitly without question, and honor all other gull-hawks as their rank required.

No, this was not the time for silliness, games, mock disrespect, or any inappropriate behavior that might be allowable out in the field. Although the most important tests occurred tomorrow, Frederick felt that the Messenger had already begun the Wing's evaluation. And, as if he could read Frederick's mind, the Messenger spoke:

"Hidden Beach will be your home for the next few days, until the Call is over. You will be sequestered here. No guard will be posted, yet you are not allowed to leave the boundaries of the beach. You may fly within these boundaries, but only to a height of one hundred feet. In addition, you will observe the rules of silence from sundown tonight until I arrive again in the morning. Are these rules understood?"

Frederick answered affirmatively for the Wing, and the Messenger continued, "The Call will begin tomorrow morning when the Sun reaches directly above SkyToucher Mountain. I will return shortly before then, when the sun crosses the valley, and explain what is expected of you. But know in your hearts that no matter what I tell you in the morning, if your flight and faith are not true, you will fail. I trust that your faith in Krystos, your teachers, and your Commander have prepared you for the two Tests of the Call." The Messenger paused for a moment, his gaze sweeping left and right, looking at the entire Wing. "Please bow your heads:

"Our Most High Creator, we confess our sins.
Please forgive us with your kind heart,
And extend to us your boundless grace.

Guide us in all we do, in flying and faith,
Help us to search our hearts and minds
And burn away any impure feelings and thoughts,
With the power and wisdom of your Sacred Spirit.
We say this prayer in the name and through the
    power
Of Krystos, your only begotten Son, the Messiah and
    Savior.
Amen."

"They are here, Apostle," said the Messenger. "As you instructed, they're sequestered at Hidden Beach, under strict orders to stay put, and remain silent from sundown— until I return tomorrow."

"Very good, Messenger," replied the Apostle. "Any unusual occurrences on the flight?"

The Messenger looked down, wiping his face with his wing. "Apostle, there was this one thing."

"Oh?"

"Just before we turned inland, a dozen Blackhawks crossed our flight path. Your Excellency, this is indeed a very rare event, and could be a sign of great good, or great evil!"

"Leave the interpretation of this event to the High Council," replied the Apostle sternly. Realizing his overstatement he softened, "I am sorry, Messenger. You may have interpreted the Blackhawk sighting correctly. It is indeed true that the Call is a crucible of both good and evil, and it is up to us, with the guidance of the Most High, to separate the good from the evil, the truth from the heresy. Thank you, Messenger, you may go now."

As the Messenger walked out of the inner chamber, the Apostle turned toward the twelve High Council Elders.

"We have another sign, Council. What does each of you interpret the Blackhawk crossing to mean?"

"It is clear to me—the Call is righteous," said Nicholas.

"There is definitely evil within that Wing; the entire 77th may need to be excommunicated—in its entirety," warned Gabriel.

"We have a choice to make between good and evil, and they are intertwined," voiced Samuel.

Olivia watched the proceedings, unwilling to reveal her mixed emotions about the Call and this intriguing sign. Her thoughts on the Blackhawk encounter were that it showed divine presence around Frederick and his Wing. *Something is happening here, which is larger than the Council fathomed!* She wanted to speak up, but chose not to. The politics against the 77th and Frederick welled too strong right now.

"Any other ideas, impressions, feelings?" Asked the Apostle. "Patrick?"

"I am greatly disturbed," said Patrick, staunch and tireless defender of the faith. "Every place we turn, another so-called mystical happening occurs around Frederick. He is dangerous, and at the least must be removed from command, from Triumvirate, and from any position of authority or influence. We do not need a cult forming around another misguided mystic. Our sacred Traditions are clear—nothing is to be added to the Teachings, they are perfect in themselves. If Frederick fails the Call, then we'll have a clear sign, and I will vote for his immediate excommunication!"

Concerned about Patrick's bold declaration, and the chorus of agreement that followed, Olivia had to speak up.

However, she had to pick her words very carefully, her position tenuous.

"Apostle and Elders, hear me!" Since Olivia rarely spoke at Council meetings, heads turned quickly her direction. The Apostle nodded her way, and she spoke, "Elder Patrick has spoken truly about our Traditions, and is wise to see the potential harm. But remember that Frederick is one of our top commanders, has proved himself in battle, in faith, and in leadership for a number of years. Before the reports of the unexplained events reached us, he was in line for promotion, and viewed as a potential Elder. Please, we must not judge him and the 77th before the Call. The Blackhawk sign could be telling us that Frederick's fate hangs in the balance. Perhaps Frederick is being Called because he needs the chance to prove his true nature. Maybe that is why he is being brought before us."

"And if he fails the Call? What do you think we should do then?" challenged Patrick, upset that Olivia had shifted the discussion, and squelched his momentum.

"It will depend upon the failure," replied Olivia smoothly. "The rules are straightforward—a minor error will be cause for demotion. However, Patrick, be clear that if Frederick blasphemes, then the course you have suggested—excommunication—may be appropriate and completely justified. I, however, will not pre-judge him, or his Wing. Let the Call's Test of True Flight and Test of True Faith separate the righteous from the wicked, truth from error; only at that point, when we've seen the results, will we know how to proceed.

"Thank you for your wise words, High Council," said the Apostle, adroitly cutting off further discussion. "This problem has been with us for the past few months, and

I have spent many hours in prayer about it, and about Frederick. My interpretation of the Blackhawk crossing is that indeed we have a mixture of good and evil in this situation. There is good and evil in the Flock, just as there is good and evil in Frederick. There is good and evil in each of us as well. That is our spiritual nature.

"However, I believe that the problems within the 77th come from Frederick's misguided mysticism, and despite his outstanding record, and his potential in Triumvirate, there is a something amiss within him. The Call will expose whatever is hidden, and if evil is present, we'll exorcize it. If Frederick passes the Call, and thus is redeemed, then it could be that he'll retain his command, and remain on the list of potential Elders. I've met him, conversed with him, spent time with him. Make no mistake about it; there is a strong part of him that resonates with the Most High. I, for one, have not given up on our 77th Wing Commander."

"But if Frederick fails the Call, and evil is found in him, then we will come down on him hard, without pity!" The Apostle took a deep breath, looking around the room.

"Prepare yourself tonight, Elders, for tomorrow you must judge most righteously. Although there has been no Call performed for a long time, you should know what is expected of you. I ask that you remain in prayer, in close communion with the Most High until you sleep, and begin immediately again in the morning. Convene here just before the sun reaches SkyToucher," finished the Apostle, gesturing at the snow-capped mountain, which dominated the southeastern sky.

As the Elders walked out of the chamber, the Apostle called out, "Patrick, Olivia, please, remain with me for a moment."

The Triumvirate leader looked at the two Elders, his eyes intense. They waited, unsure of what would be said. "Each of you possesses a valid perspective. But once the Call reveals to us the truth of this matter, I want unity. Clear? This is too important to have any kind of divisiveness within the High Council. Put your personal feelings aside and judge as the Son would judge, with spiritual righteousness—and love! Although each gull-hawk is important, keep in mind the Flock—what will be best for the Flock, not just today, but over a vast expanse of time. Triumvirate has survived and prospered and tended our Flock for one hundred generations, by the grace of the Most High. Do you understand the awesome responsibility you have been given?" They both nodded, quiet under the Triumvirate leader's stern gaze. "All right, then, go forth, and remember to pray. We need it!"

Patrick flew away, but his anger still smoldered. *I didn't deserve that little pep talk! There is no question that Frederick should be sacrificed for the good of the Flock. Triumvirate must maintain authority and discipline with our Teaching, no deviations permitted.* He stroked powerfully, channeling his frustration into a steep climb. Off to his left Patrick spied Olivia winging her way home. *How dare she question me! I should be the next Apostle after all, not some . . . some female! I'll keep my eye on her, that's for sure.* He glided toward his resting place, grim but smug, certain of his faith in the Most High, and favored status.

Frederick spent a restless night of semi-sleep, waking and dozing under the star-filled sky. Dreams filled the patches of sleep, dreams of Blackhawks, Olivia, and flying, all jumbled up, mixed together, with fear and uncertainty permeating all. When the dawn came, Frederick felt tired and angry for not getting a good night's rest. *Great! Here it is, the most important day of my life, and I can't even get decent sleep. Oh Most High, please help me today—I really, really need it!*

The 77th Wing Commander cut off the unproductive, melancholy thought-path and looked around. His Wing still slept, so he flew up to an oversized boulder perched near the boundary that the Messenger had established. Frederick began his morning prayer and meditation, sinking inside himself, into the origin of his mind. Focusing on breath, he drifted down, down into the depth of his soul.

Sunlight streaming over the land brought Frederick back to consciousness. A warm sense of peace enveloped him, and he felt stronger, surer, more confident. *Thank you, Most High, I feel your presence, and I am grateful. And thank you for the beautiful sunrise.*

With that thought, he turned around and surveyed his Wing. A few were stirring; Gregory strolled along the water's edge in a walking meditation. Spying Frederick, the 77th First Officer joined his commander. Gregory looked in Frederick's eyes, and saw peace and assurance gleaming forth. He nodded at Frederick, turned toward the sun, and began a centering prayer. As the rest of the Wing awoke, many glanced up and saw their two leaders on the rock, and knew that all was well, for the moment, anyway. As the sun approached SkyToucher, the Messenger flew in; his elite four gull-hawk escort team close behind, landed on the sandy beach, and addressed the Wing.

"You are to follow me to the feeding grounds—once there we'll recite the morning prayer and you'll be allowed to eat. Then we will fly to Home Beach where you will receive further instruction, and face the beginning of the Call. Although the time of silence is over, the Council recommends that you keep words to a minimum, and stay focused on the tests ahead. Commander Frederick, bring the Wing in behind me."

"Gull-hawks, listen carefully!" The Messenger's voice boomed forcefully across Home Beach. He pointed to a distinctive rock that towered above a wide, rocky ledge near the center of Home Beach. "Hear and follow our Apostle, head of the High Council, leader of Triumvirate."

The gathered gull-hawks hushed. In a moment the only sound heard were small waves breaking gently on the beach below. The Apostle stepped forward; behind him stood the High Council, Olivia among them. The Apostle perched on the raised, weathered outcropping, perfect for gatherings such as this. Off to each side of the Apostle and High Council stood an elite squad of Triumvirate warrior gull-hawks. Above the outcropping a small cliff rose sharply. Stationed at the top was an entire wing, the 1st, Triumvirate's highest ranking warriors, elite of elites. Situated on each side of the outcropping were additional squads of warrior gull-hawks. Finally, four Wings flew patrol in each of the four directions. Not that the Apostle or the Council needed such overwhelming protection. No, the gull-hawks of the 77th and every other wing were so well trained—some might even say brainwashed—that no thought of revolt existed in a Triumvirate gull-hawk's mind. Nonetheless, a show of strength reinforced the power of the Apostle and his High Council; they commanded respect, obedience, and submission.

Frederick's Wing was herded onto the white sand in front of the Apostle's outcropping. The sandy beach, wide and long, could hold many wings and thousands of gull-hawks, and more so during low tide. This was Home Beach, where Triumvirate gathered the Flock for holy days, celebrations, and rarely, a Call of Confidence. Today, though, besides the Apostle, the Elders, the warrior gull-hawks, and Frederick's Wing, regulars were conspicuously absent. The area had been cleared of all except those directly involved by order of the Apostle. No one else could witness the Call, for it was to be feared, and awed, and forever remain a mystery to all but the chosen few.

"Elders, gull-hawks of the 1st, the 2nd, and the 77th Wing, hear my prayer. Oh Most High, we implore you to guide us today, to shine the light of truth upon us, and help us judge wisely. May we be filled with the Holy Spirit in mind, heart and soul. In the name of your Son, Krystos Gull-hawk, Amen."

The Apostle paused, and then led the gull-hawks in the morning meditation. Afterwards, he spoke directly to the 77th Wing.

"You have journeyed far from your assigned post at the High Council's request to participate in the Call of Confidence. You have been Called because of reports of unusual events and teachings occurring in and around the 77th Wing. Stories strange enough to have reached us here at Home Beach.

"Reports and stories are not enough to excommunicate a fellow gull-hawk, but what we've heard has us concerned enough to bring you in for an intensive examination and review. Your commander, Frederick, will experience the most scrutiny since the reports center around him. Nonetheless, you all must undergo the Call so we may determine if your faith is pure—if you are truly gull-hawks worthy of being called Triumvirate.

"The Call is divided into two parts. The first part is named 'The Test of True Flight.' The Wing will be judged as a whole, and each of you will be judged individually, judged how well you fly in accordance with the Teachings. Since flight is a reflection of your soul, the way you fly will help us to see what is in your soul.

"The second part is named 'The Test of True Faith.' You will be individually sequestered and interrogated during this test. There will be no help from your fellow gull-hawks. Each of you will be questioned by two of the Elders, and two other Triumvirate gull-hawks will be present as special witnesses. You will be asked to discuss the teachings of Triumvirate, the Most High, and the Son. Your faith will be revealed; we will know if you carry any heresy in your mind, and if so, whether you can repent truly from the infestation of falsehood in your heart.

"We *must* weed out heresy whenever and wherever it exists. The Call has *never* failed to identify heretical thinkers. I pray that you succeed, and you can, if it is the will of the Most High. Some Wings who've gone through the Call and judged pure have continued on to greatness. The 77th will not be stigmatized if you succeed.

"But the Call does exude tremendous pressure, and the weak minded are vulnerable. It's rare, but a few have passed the Call, but ended up leaving Triumvirate prematurely. Those particular gull-hawks could not shake off the deep probing, and later struggled to rise above the overwhelming exposure experienced during the Call.

"If a gull-hawk fails the Call he, or she, will be punished. On occasion, that punishment has been quite harsh—banishment from the Flock by excommunication!"

The Apostle paused, letting his warning sink in. Frederick glanced at Gregory, their eyes meeting momentarily. The Wing Commander shook his head imperceptibly, while Gregory grimaced. They turned back toward the Apostle as he began again.

"While an individual can suffer significantly from failing the Call, there are additional, harsh consequences. Gull-hawks of the 77th, hear me. A failure by one means a failure by the Wing. Everyone fails, the entire 77th." Two tests, one result. All must pass, or all will fail.

"The Call is severe, you knew that before, and now you know the full truth, the complete interdependence of your achievement—or—failure." The Apostle's gaze settled squarely on Frederick. The Wing Commander fought back a shudder, but could not stop a terrible foreboding curling around his gut. He nodded his understanding to the Apostle, hoping that was all the Apostle could see.

The Triumvirate leader brought his focus back to the Wing as a whole and finished with a positive tone, "May the Most High bless the 77th in its entirety and each of you individually, and guide you during this most difficult time. And, may Krystos infuse each of the Elders with true spiritual discernment."

The Apostle stopped, looked up towards the sky, as if saying a silent prayer to the Most High. He stepped back to his sacred place at the middle of the Apostle`s Rock. The original Messenger gull-hawk, now revealed as High Council Elder Jeremiah, stepped forward and provided more details to the 77th Wing about the Test of True Flight.

Frederick waited nervously, anxious to begin, uncertain about his chances, especially after the Apostle reiterated about how accurate the Call was in rooting out heresy. And more importantly, that all must pass the Call, or all would fail! Frederick shook off these negative thoughts and focused on the Elder's instructions. Each gull-hawk would go off with two High Council Elders, a recorder and a squad of warrior gull-hawks; the Elders would judge the gull-hawk's ability, the recorder gull-hawk would record the judgment, and the warrior gull-hawks would ensure order.

Elder Jeremiah explained that The Test of True Flight spanned several days, given that one hundred sixty-two gull-hawks had to be separately evaluated. After each gull-hawk had been judged, then the whole Wing would fly together, and be judged together. The results from the Test of True Flight would be kept secret until the very end of both tests. Once the Test of True Flight was complete, the Test of True Faith began. Elder Jeremiah told the Wing that more would be revealed about the second and final of the two Tests later, and then gave way to the Apostle.

"There is enough to be concerned about with the Test of True Flight, gull-hawks of the 77th. There is much to be concerned about, certainly, but mind your discipline and stay focused. The consequences of the Call will affect you for not only this lifetime, but quite possibly . . . " Here the Apostle paused as he slowly scanned back and forth, eyeing the 77th with his usual mixture of intensity and compassion. The Triumvirate supreme commander finally halted, his gaze once again focused on Frederick, "quite possibly, you could be affected for not just this life, but for *all* Eternity!"

Chapter Six

I~N SILENCE, SIX GULL-HAWKS~ were escorted down the beach.

Frederick assumed that these six had been chosen randomly, and he also assumed that he and the command team would be tested last, but did not know why he knew this. He watched as six of the 77th Wing, six of his loyal gull-hawks disappeared off into the distance. He had a pretty good idea about what the individual Test of True Flight would be comprised off. It would most definitely start with level flight, followed by thermal climbing, soaring, diving, landing, flying motionless, acrobatics, and combat maneuvering. Frederick looked around as he finished the thought; saw Gregory with his eyes closed. A long wait stretched out before those not yet chosen, and Gregory appeared to be in quiet prayer.

Frederick took the hint and joined him.

Throughout the day gull-hawks came and went, with only a short break for food allowed. As dusk fell over the beach, the Apostle and his entourage returned. A second group of gull-hawks also returned at about the same time—the Elder judges, the recorders, the escort warrior gull-hawks, and six of the 77th. As all the gull-hawks were gathered together again, the Apostle led the evening prayer, and informed the Wing that individual tests would be completed by the next evening. That was all. Nothing more would be—or need to be—spoken.

Sundown turned to dusk and then nightfall, with end-less stars twinkling on the cloudless, moonless evening. Frederick gazed across the sky and marveled at the mist-like white background that seemed to float above and beyond the stars. The nature of the stars and the white mist had been hotly debated over the generations; some said the stars were fires in the sky; others insisted they were cousins of the one sun that warmed all creation. The white background was thought by many to be a great cloud that fed the stars—the Most High's manna. The Triumvirate's official position on the stars: they were the some of the many eyes of the Creator, and demonstrated the omni-presence of the Most High. Nothing was hidden, even in the dark, for the Most High has more eyes than can be counted. The white cloud-like substance, according to the official teachings of Triumvirate, could only be the physi-cal manifestation of the Almighty's Sacred Spirit. Along with Frederick's questions on some of Triumvirate's doc-trine, he also thought something was missing from their teachings on the physical sciences.

This feeling nagged at him again, and the uncertainty gnawed away at his self-confidence. *How much more was wrong with Triumvirate? Most High, how do I find the truth, find a clear flight path?*

He shook himself, inadvertently startling Gregory. Frederick winked at his friend—the 77th's second-in-com-mand, and Gregory shot his commander a questioning gaze, then a brief smile, barely visible in the dark night. Gregory re-closed his eyes, and Frederick followed, still-ing his internal dialogue in meditation.

The sunrise startled Frederick awake, just as he dreamed of approaching a great, engrossing, compassionate white light. Unconditional love emanated from this ethereal light, and the sudden loss of it saddened the young gull-hawk, the withdrawal tangible despite its dream origin.

Any further mourning was cut short, however, by the approach of the Messenger Elder. After morning prayers, the gull-hawks were allowed to feed, and then the individual tests of true flight resumed. Six by six, Frederick watched the remainder of his Wing fly off with their inquisitors. By mid-morning, only Frederick and his command team remained, and they huddled together, anxious, tension high. Nathan eyed Frederick with a worried look. Frederick nodded slowly and flashed a tight grin, trying his best to reassure the healer. He gave Nathan the signal to go within, the ancient sign that identified a fellow believer to another back in the days of persecution, one hundred generations ago. Nathan nodded, understanding coming quickly to the bright, young healer gull-hawk.

Soon the Elders and escort warrior gull-hawks reappeared with the last of the Wing. Two Elders came to each of the command team, and took them off. This time Frederick saw Olivia, and his heart jumped! For an instant she looked at Frederick, and compassion filled her eyes, replaced an instant later with a blank stare. She turned abruptly away, not wanting to alert anyone to their brief connection. Frederick's escort came up to next him, and he followed behind and between them as they took off. His heart pounded nervously, and he felt a surge of fear. *I don't want to fail, Most High!* He faltered, but regained enough composure to stay with his escorts. Frederick prayed to the Creator—and Krystos—asking once again for guidance, comfort, mercy and strength in this moment of crisis.

They arrived at a pre-arranged point, landing on the deserted stretch of Home Beach. One of the Elders spoke to Frederick, "You will demonstrate to us your flying ability. You will be successful at this Test if you fly in the Way that the Son flew—the same way that you were taught by Triumvirate. You'll begin with level flight, then climbing, soaring, diving and landing. You'll start again with level flight but this time will climb until you can attain enough lift to remain motionless; you must remain motionless until we advise you to stop. Then you will perform the level five acrobatics - triple loop, inverted roll, power dive, and snap turn. Repeat back to me your Test of True Flight, Commander Frederick."

Frederick made a sign, indicating that he was not allowed to speak.

"Very good, Frederick, you have passed a hidden test by not replying. You've permission to speak—please recite to me what the instructions for the Test are."

Frederick repeated the Test back, without hesitation, his mind now clear and memory clicking. The Test of True Flight was quite similar to the elite warrior gull-hawk final training routine, which Joram had put him through several times. It would be a difficult routine, made all that more challenging from the pressure of the watchful presence of the judging Elders and the Recorder. Failure was unthinkable—he would succeed!

Frederick took off, leading the way, the Elders on each side, the Recorder smoothly behind. Frederick flew without problem through the first part of the test, then, rode a thermal up to a strong air current. There he initiated his period of motionlessness, shaping his wings and body perfectly to remain stationary. He watched the Elders, waiting for their signal that he had achieved sufficient time. When he saw them both nod, he wheeled about, initiating the acrobatic part of the Test. Here he reveled—looping, diving, and turning. The countless hours of practice, the discipline to put himself and his Wing through grueling exercises—recently and over the past several years—paid off as he knifed through the air in a final power dive, finishing off with a glorious landing. He wiped the smile off his face, suddenly afraid of failing due to some imagined disrespect.

The two Elders landed beside him, informing Frederick that his Test of True Flight was finished. They flew back to Hidden Beach, and Frederick could see that he was the last to return, the final gull-hawk to complete the individual test. He assembled with the rest of the 77th, and one of the Elders spoke to the Wing.

"Now is the time for the Test of True Flight for the entire Wing. The silence directive is lifted as to flying commands only; but other than those command words, no talking is allowed. You will follow the same formation order as in the individual flight tests; in addition, the Wing will be required to perform these formations: Traditional, Victory, Sacrifice, Defender, Redemption, Resurrection and Ascension.

"All twelve Elders will be present and shall judge the Wing. In addition, the Apostle will also observe, and can add his judgment if he so desires. As before, it will be your faith, your deepest truth, combined with your flying skill, which will determine the outcome of the Test. Commander Frederick, please assemble your Wing, and begin with level flight."

Frederick pushed aside the thought that Olivia would be among his judges and brought his Wing into formation.

He gave brief instructions and quickly led the 77th along the beach in level flight, just has he had done so for the previous week of intensive training, and the months of drills prior to that. Frederick used the southeasterly wind to bring the Wing into a steep climb, followed by soaring, diving, skimming and landing. The Elders flew above and below the Wing, but Frederick paid them no attention, no heed. For a moment it seemed as if they were back at the Cliff, enjoying flying for the sheer love of it.

After the superbly executed landing, the 77th climbed high into the sky and began the required period of motion-lessness. Here Frederick did pay attention to the Elders, watching them for the signal that his Wing had achieved motionlessness for the proper amount of time. After the signal, the acrobatics began.

It was quite a spectacle witnessing one hundred sixty-two gull-hawks doing a triple loop as one. Olivia, flying well above, marveled at the 77th's precision and synchron-icity. Although the Elders had not compiled any of the Test results, from what she had seen so far in the individual Tests and this demonstration, Frederick's Wing was per-forming well. Olivia had a delicate balance to achieve; she must perform her role as Elder and judge according to the Law while simultaneously wanted dearly for Frederick and his Wing to pass this most difficult of tests. It would not be enough for Frederick and the 77th to just *barely* pass. No! If Frederick was to regain respect and rise in the Flock, the Wing must pass with high marks. In fact, if the 77th passed with clear success, it was conceivable that Frederick might rise faster in the Flock than if he had not been Called, since all doubts about his ability—and espe-cially his faith—would be stilled. Olivia had considered all of this several times before in the days leading up to the Call, but her hope had gained momentum as she watched the flawless performance of the 77th, led by their commander, Frederick, the gull-hawk she loved.

The Wing moved seamlessly into the Traditional formation once the last acrobatic maneuver finished. After a signal from the lead Elder, Frederick squawked the command to form up in Victory. Successfully completing this formation, the Wing performed in order: Sacrifice, Defender, Redemption, Resurrection and finally, Ascension.

The last week of intense training, combined with the normal daily instruction, repetition and a standard of excellence bordering on impeccability seemed to be paying off for the 77th. Even the Apostle, watching from below on the sacred beach, was awed by this display of the Triumvirate's time-honed formations. Despite Frederick's questioning of some of Triumvirate's exclusionary teachings, he nonetheless followed the Son as rigorously as any, and stridently taught the 77th about self-control and responsibility, love and spirit. A compassionate heart, a focused mind, a disciplined body and a loving spirit comprised a typical 77th gull-hawk after the mandatory minimum one year of training was completed. Many initiate gull-hawks volunteered to serve in the 77th, despite the Wing's reputation for a grueling and demanding training schedule. And when the yearlong enlistment was complete, the 77th gull-hawk graduates typically had their choice among the many paths available in the Triumvirate.

Yes, Frederick had achieved this distinction in just a few years of being Commander. The Apostle, reflecting on Frederick's reputation for being an outstanding teacher with the rumors about possible heresy, puzzled on the paradox that was the 77th commander. *The Call will extrude out the heresy, if it exists. It is a powerful weapon against an imposter, no matter what is said or taught. The intense steps of the Call will distill truth, and the dregs, if any, will be easily identified.*

The Apostle shook off his thoughts and looked up in time to see the 77th move from the Resurrection formation into Ascension. The Wing began with level flight, seeking a powerful updraft. The uncertainty of locating a strong enough updraft, either from a thermal or ridge lift, made the Ascension formation risky, unpredictable. Ascension was used in peacetime to inspire the faithful and in battle to rally the fighting gull-hawks. To watch one hundred sixty-two gull-hawks shoot upward like a geyser, have the twelve squads peel off in twelve directions, leaving the command team to continue up as high as they could, was to witness a powerful, awe-inspiring event.

The Apostle recalled the beginning of Ascension as the 77th began. A great battle with Shahadah over the sacred Island of Eternal Peace was apparently over, with the Flock's losses high and position grim. Desperate, the Flock leader gathered his commanders and prayed for guidance. As the legend goes, an image, or vision came to Patraenus, the Flock leader who had actually followed Krystos. He saw the Son, rising straight up into the air, headed towards the Most High, saying *follow me, my gull-hawks, follow me.* Patraenus shared his vision, and it was Catharsis, his second-in-command, who translated the vision into a practical plan. "We must motivate and unite the gull-hawks, and at the same time, strike fear into the enemy."

And so the Ascension formation was birthed. Catharsis explained to Patraenus his idea, to have the main formation ascend up to the sky, turn around, and using the momentum of the great height achieved, plunge into the middle of the Shahadah command team. Patraenus agreed, and sent messengers to the nearest wings to follow Patraenus and his First Wing. The Shahadah were momentarily transfixed by the sight of Wing after Wing ascending straight up into the air. Impossible, they thought, how are they getting the lift? Was El-Rah providing the mysterious power to ascend so quickly? Before they could recover, Patraenus' First Wing shattered through the Shahadah leaders. Those wings following immediately behind smashed holes in the Shahadah formations. The remaining Wings, inspired by the incredible turn of events, rose together, fought ferociously and finished off the enemy forces. Triumvirate won the day and with momentum gloriously shifted, prevailed in the war, wrenching back control of the Island of Eternal Peace. All of those moments—almost one hundred generations ago—where recorded in the Sacred Teachings, and had become imbedded in the Triumvirate consciousness as well as integral to their "true" way of flying.

The Apostle watched the 77th complete a flawless Ascension formation and glide into Home Beach. Breathing a sigh of relief, Frederick glanced at the Apostle and waited for a signal, a command, or some kind of directive. Receiving none, he led the Wing into a landing and, with Gregory's help, brought them to attention. All of the Elders, Recorders, and Warrior gull-hawks also landed and returned to their respective places. Almost simultaneously, each turned to the Apostle, who surveyed the Home Beach, the gull-hawks, and the moment.

"The test of True Flight is finished. The Elders, Recorders and I will now meet to review and judge each of you, and the Wing as a whole, while you are escorted to your feeding place. The command of silence remains in effect—no exceptions! After your meal the Wing will return to Home Beach and wait for the Test of True Faith. When the second Test is complete, we will again assemble as a group and . . . " he looked over the Wing, his eyes stern, his voice ringing with authority, "announce the *final* results." The Apostle paused, and then continued:

"May your faith be strong enough, and true enough, to sustain you, and if not, may the Most High have mercy on your soul."

His encouragement—and warning—given, the Apostle turned from the Wing, gathered the Elders and Recorders, and proceeded to the back of the sacred rock ledge. Jeremiah, escorted by a squad of Elite gull-hawks, approached Frederick and motioned for him and his Wing to follow. The gull-hawks fed hungrily, the effects of the physically and emotionally demanding day felt by all. With bellies filled, and spirits somewhat replenished, the 77th made its way back to Hidden Beach and awaited the second and final Test. When a short time later six of his Wing was again taken, Frederick felt anxiety resurface— the silent yet relentless gnawing at his soul.

Six by six, six by six; Frederick watched them leave to be tested. When they returned, those tested were segregated from those who had not yet been subjected to the questions, the inquisition. While this segregation was understandable, it upset Frederick since it broke up his Wing. But truly, this was just a minor irritation. The real problem, the deep anxiety awaited in the queries to be asked, and the imperial, authoritative attitude of those who asked the question.

Frederick had an idea about the nature of the questions that would be thrust upon him after his discussion with Joram and Dayleen. Most would be easy since Frederick knew the Triumvirate Sacred Traditions and Doctrine better than most. No, what really scared the young gull-hawk was one basic, perplexing question. It would be asked—no doubt—but how it would be posed might make the difference towards him answering with an acceptable response.

Do you agree that the Triumvirate Traditions and Doctrine are the ONLY way to salvation? The correct answer was an immediate, unswerving YES! For Frederick, however, it was not so simple. His answer, from the depth of his being, his deepest intuition, where his soul merged with the Most High, was—NO!

He had been raised in Triumvirate's Sacred Traditions, the Most High watching over all, the inability for gull-hawks to find redemption and salvation from the Most High on their own, belief in Krystos's great sacrifice for all gull-hawks, and the necessity of surrender to the Son and Most High in order to attain salvation in this life and immortality in the life to come. And Frederick knew that this Way worked, it truly worked, and was indeed a true path to salvation. But the *only* way? Here, he was skeptical, unsure. Joram and Dayleen, although not talking about it directly, had hinted about other paths to the Most High.

More importantly, Frederick had experienced glimpses of Shahadah—Malibakr's faith; the faith of the SouthLand Flock—during their brief time together. Even now he re-membered Malibakr's family's intense but compassionate faith. They did not seem to need Krystos . . . Shahadah gull-hawks had already surrendered to El-Rah, the name

127

they gave the Most High. Of course Malibakr's family suggested that Shahadah was the only true way. That claim to exclusivity was one of Triumvirate and Shahadah's remarkable similarities, and paradoxes. How could both be right? *So who am I to believe that Triumvirate Traditions are all true and thus any others, especially Shahadah, were wrong? Or visa versa? Can I honestly say that only my Triumvirate Way is true? Others can say it without doubt, but can I?*

And yet, the spiritual teachings of Triumvirate were unwavering against all other "ways." Although Shahadah beliefs may contain some bits of truth, the truth—according to Triumvirate—had been placed there by the Evil One to deceive true believers. Since the fundamental belief in Krystos as savior and Son of the Most High was missing from Shahadah, then it ultimately failed as the truthful path. But how could Frederick really know if Shahadah—or any other spiritual path—did fail? The Most High knew for sure, and probably the Son, the *real* Krystos who flew the sky one hundred generations ago, not the Krystos which Triumvirate selectively presented as "real." Did all gull-hawks find "the truth" at the moment of death? Triumvirate taught that they did, although their doctrine was that believers went on to live for eternity with the Most High while non-believers were cast into utter darkness, tormented forever by the Evil One. To enter paradise, a believer had to accept Krystos as Savior of the world, the *only* Son of the Most High.

Although he had thought it fortunate at the time, just now it seemed quite unfortunate that Frederick had saved Malibakr in his adolescence so many moons before. That chance encounter had opened Frederick's mind and heart to another Flock's belief system. Frederick had experienced firsthand Malibakr's deep faith and disciple, his depth of commitment and love for his SouthLand Flock. And that love was shared unconditionally with Frederick, too, and Frederick had returned it. How could Frederick honestly say that Shahadah was not a true path? And, according to Malibakr, Shahadah was in reality the one true path, not Triumvirate. When pressed, Malibakr had admitted that Triumvirate Sacred Traditions contained much truth and members of Triumvirate's Flock were not totally evil. In fact, Shahadah revered Krystos as a true prophet of El-Rah, but not the Savior or Son of the Most High, in addition to a number of other common roots and basic beliefs. Nonetheless, to Malibakr, and all Shahadah gull-hawks, Triumvirate teachings on faith and the spiritual path came up short, and would not reconcile gull-hawks to El-Rah, the Most High. Only the Shahadah way would do that.

At this point Frederick was skeptical about the *exclusive* claims of either Flock. What truly mattered to him was whether the practice of the Way—either Triumvirate or Shahadah—or perhaps another, unknown spiritual tradition, changed a gull-hawk from a squawking, selfish, undisciplined and insensitive gull-hawk to a loving, faithful, discerning, compassionate and spiritual gull-hawk. And the best example of such a gull-hawk was Krystos! Krystos, initially deemed the Messiah, and later called the Son of the Most High by Triumvirate, had lived his life fully, completely, and unselfishly. According to the Sacred Traditions, he could outfly anyone, he healed the sick, could calm storms, and even read minds. He had, in fact, given his life up rather than compromise who he was and his destiny. There existed little if any exclusionary rhetoric in the one oral Tradition passed down about

Krystos. The authenticity of what had survived from the early Tradition was hotly debated within the learned centers of Triumvirate; however, the every day gull-hawk had been shielded from much of this contentious, perpetual debate. The exclusionary dogma—from either Triumvirate or Shahadah, was wrong, in Frederick's opinion. These thoughts had been repeated countless times inside his brain, and once again swirled through him; broken off only when the Elder/Messenger called out.

"Command Team—front and center. It is now your turn for the Test!"

Frederick was escorted north of Home Beach to a small stretch of sand surrounded by craggy rocks on three sides and a gentle bay on the fourth. Two Elders stood quietly, a Recorder gull-hawk, and one other gull-hawk whom Frederick could not identify. His heart rate quickened as the warrior gull-hawk escorts left the immediate area, leaving Frederick with the four, alone.

"Stand here, Frederick Gull-hawk, your Test of True Faith is about to commence. You will be required to recite the Basic Doctrine—the same as what all conferees recite upon their initiation as full members of Triumvirate. The only difference between then and now is the truth of your words will be verified by the gull-hawk standing on our right here. You may have heard of the Council's mysterious ability to discern the truth when questioning a gull-hawk. The mystery is revealed only to a few, of which you are now one. And, Frederick, you are charged and commanded to say *nothing* of the details of this Test to others, including the existence of these special gull-hawks, known as Truth Seekers.

The Elder reinforced the point with a stern look at the

77th Wing Commander. Frederick nodded in return, and the Elder continued: "Although we Elders are the judges, the Truth Seeker plays a special role. His job is to listen to your responses to our questions. He was specially bred, then trained since birth to listen, to listen and watch, to listen and watch carefully, closely, and astutely to the gull-hawk being questioned, totally focused, without distraction. Movements, breathing, voice fluctuations and tone are absorbed and analyzed by the Truth Seeker. A gull-hawk under this intense, single-minded scrutiny is motivated to speak truth, and, if not, the Truth Seeker knows without doubt when a lie has been told, whether a "white-lie," a "half-truth," or just a plain old, absolute deceitful lie. In essence, he is the eyes and ears of the Most High.

"And so I caution you, Frederick, to speak only the complete, full truth. You will begin by reciting the Basic Doctrine and the Original Commandments. Then, we will ask you several questions which will help reveal to us the your deepest, most hidden beliefs. When these questions are answered to our satisfaction, the Test will be complete. Please begin, now . . . "

Frederick closed his eyes, took a measured breath, and began reciting the twelve commandments:

"Worship only the Most High; do not worship
    material things;
Do not call upon the Most High without true need;
Set aside one day each week, and dedicate it to the
    Most High;
Honor your parents, and your grandparents, and all
    of those who came before you;
Do not kill unless to sustain or defend yourself or

your Flock;

Be true in your heart, your mind and your body with
your mate;

Do not steal from your neighbor;

Speak honestly; do not lie—nothing is hidden from
the Most High;

Do not covet what belongs to another gull-hawk;

Do unto others, as you would have them do unto
you;

Love the Most High with all your heart, soul and
mind; and

Love one another as Krystos loved you."

Frederick paused, looked at each of the Elders, and continued: "The Most High created the world, and gave the
gull-hawk a very special place in it. Originally, the first
two gull-hawks could speak directly to the Most High, but
they disobeyed Him, and were cast out of this special place
and lost their ability to talk directly with the Most High.
After many generations of struggle, toil, and a mixture of
deep faithfulness and shallow foolishness by gull-hawks,
the Most High once again showed mercy and sent us his
only begotten Son, Krystos, to show us how to live, and
ultimately to sacrifice himself so that gull-hawks could be
redeemed and reconciled. He brings back to gull-hawks the
image of the Most High in which gull-hawks were made,
but which gull-hawks had lost. Krystos, infused with the
Spirit of the Most High, fulfilled prophecy, performed
many miracles in addition to sharing with us the Sacred
Tradition. Even through the Son suffered a horrible death
by fellow gull-hawks; he escaped this death due to his purity, his divine nature, and was resurrected. The Most High

raised Krystos's gull-hawk body from the dead and eventually Krystos ascended directly back to the Most High.

"If you believe in Krystos, believe with all of your heart that he was the Son of the Most High and died for our sins, and you surrender your will—your life—to Him, then you will be saved. This is the first step in a spiritual journey, but it is an indispensable one just the same. Daily surrender, prayer, reciting or listening to the Sacred Tradition (which came from the Spirit of the Most High, and given to the founders of Triumvirate to carry to all Flocks) and doing the will of the Son are critical ingredients to living a victorious life, to glorifying the Son and the Most High in thought, word and deed."

Frederick took another deep breath, exhaled slowly, and glanced at both Elders, then the Recorder, and finally, reluctantly, at the Truth Seeker. The Truth Seeker eyed Frederick, silent, watchful, his eyes mirrors to Frederick's soul.

Frederick shuddered; feeling exposed all at once under the steady gaze of the other four, especially the Truth Seeker. Fortunately for Frederick, he believed all of what he just had spoken. At the corner of his mind, however, lurked several doubts, problems and concerns he felt about the Sacred Tradition. Perhaps he'll get through the Test without having to uncover the waver in his faith. The High Council Elder cut off this hopeful thought:

"Is that it? Are you finished with your recital?"

"Yes, I am."

"Fine. Now, the questions will begin. Frederick, why did you join Triumvirate?"

Frederick did not expect this question; he thought that they would focus strictly on Sacred Tradition. He closed his eyes and thought for a few moments, casting back to his youth and his initiation into Triumvirate. So sure he had been of his future flight path, so thankful to the Most High for calling him, leading him to Triumvirate, and helping to become a full member of the Flock's guardian.

Frederick recounted this to the Elders, and that he has had a relationship with the Most High for as long as he could remember. Growing up, he watched with great admiration the quiet dignity of Triumvirate teachers, warriors and leaders. Such focused, disciplined gull-hawks! Frederick recounted the time when, in prayer, he shared with Krystos his secret desire to become a Triumvirate gull-hawk, how his prayer had seemingly been answered with an overwhelming sensation of "rightness" which flooded his very young gull-hawk body. He made known his desire and was quickly enrolled in pre-Triumvirate training. Later, Frederick learned that being a full member of Triumvirate was more that just being warrior or leader, it was actually about service to other gull-hawks, not merely about serving his own needs.

This change in purpose seemed right to the young gull-hawk, since so many of the Flock appeared to lead aimless lives in need of the Son's direction. He felt called to serve the Son and Triumvirate in whatever way was required, so when the time came to go forth and be initiated into the mysteries of Triumvirate, he went forward with no hesitation. The day Frederick had been accepted and initiated remained one of the greatest days of his life.

"I joined Triumvirate to answer a deep impulse within me. I admired the Triumvirate gull-hawks around me. Looking back, some of the reasons were for me only, self-mastery, for instance, but later it became clear that I would be one of the Most High's many warriors." Frederick paused again, indicating that he had finished the answer to this question.

"Why are you worthy to be in Triumvirate, and serve the Son and the Most High?"

"Well, there is a part of me that feels worthy to be in Triumvirate, and serve the Son and the Most High. I have dedicated my life to service, learning and teaching about the Way. I have fought battles in defense of our Flock, in defense of Triumvirate, Krystos and the Most High. That part of me is worthy. At the same time, when I stand in front of the Son, I know I'll have to answer for all of my sins and mistakes and impure thoughts. I'm a firm believer in our doctrine, 'nothing is hidden.' So in the end, I don't really know if I am worthy enough—only the Most High can judge—and answer that ultimate question."

"Would you die for the Son, and Triumvirate?"

"Yes!

"Have you ever been in such a situation?"

"I have narrowly escaped death several times in battles defending the Flock. Elders, I believe in our Way, and our cause, without hesitation."

"Do you accept the Apostle as the true representative of the Son, and his word as inspired by the Most High?"

Frederick was silent for a few moments, considering this question. He had not really thought about this. *Was the Apostle the true representative?* He had been taught that fact since he had been very young. For almost one hundred generations, a gull-hawk was selected as Apostle after careful deliberation, intense prayer, and a vote from Triumvirate High Council Elders. Frederick's few and brief experiences with the Apostle had affected him. The

Apostle seemed to be deeply spiritual, a loving yet strong presence. *If any gull-hawk was the Son's true representative, it was this gull-hawk, the Apostle.* And the words that he spoke carried significant power, and had always rang true—down to the core of Frederick's soul.

"Yes, he is the one."

"The one . . . what? Please be specific and answer the question."

Somewhat taken aback by the rebuke, Frederick replied firmly, "He is the most spiritual gull-hawk in Triumvirate. I believe that he is our best representative of the Son, and that indeed, his words are inspired by the Most High."

The Elder's eyes narrowed. "Do you believe in the Most High, the Creator of everything and do you believe in Krystos Gull-hawk, his only Son and our Savior and redeemer?"

This was a basic Triumvirate question, one asked all initiates. And yet it made him a bit nervous because of the phrase, *"only* Son." Frederick instinctively glanced over at the Truth Seeker, who returned his gaze, giving nothing away. If Krystos was the "only son," then why did His most recounted prayer he spoke with his disciples begin "OUR Father?" This puzzled Frederick, and he had recently begun to wonder about the claim whether Krystos's mother had not been impregnated by a male gull-hawk, but by the Sacred Spirit. So what was the truth? Frederick did not know, and was concerned that his lack of an immediate "yes" would indicate to the Truth Seeker that Frederick had doubts about this particular, essential doctrine. At that moment, something Joram had told him popped into Frederick's mind. It was a metaphysical translation of this Tradition. The "Only Son" was the direct offspring, the first "idea" that came forth from the Most High. Krystos fulfilled this when he flew the sky, so in that sense he was the "only" son. When each gull-hawk had achieved Krystos's level of flying, level of being, then they too would be an "only" son, or daughter, of the Most High. Joram's explanation had made sense to Frederick then, which explained that many of the stories of the Sacred Tradition were stories with a deeper, mystical meaning.

"Yes, I believe in the Most High, the Creator of everything and in Krystos Gull-hawk, his only Son and our Savior and redeemer." Frederick said firmly, and hoped that his long pause had not cost him very much.

"There is one more question, Frederick," said the Elder, apparently satisfied. He stretched his wings, and signaled the Truth Seeker to come closer, along with the Recorder and other High Council Elder. The four formed a tight circle around the young gull-hawk. Frederick felt the pressure grow, and intensify. The Elder locked his eyes upon Frederick, and recited the final question in the Call of Confidence, Test of True Faith in almost a whispered tone:

"Do you believe that all other faiths and ways fall short, that *there is only one Way to salvation,* and which is by believing in Krystos Gull-hawk, who paid with his life so that we may live reconciled with the Most High?"

Frederick took a deep breath and shivered involuntarily. At last, the dreaded question! It was the one that could bring him down, the one he had pondered in secret for several years. His mind quickly scanned for words of Joram, or thoughts of his own that could translate this question, this command into something he could say *yes* to with certainty. Frederick knew that believing in Krystos was a *true* Way to salvation, and that the only other path that Frederick knew anything about—Shahadah—had gull-hawks who believed their way was the only true path to the Most High. The Shahadah path was not the one for Frederick, and it did seem to fall short of Krystos's exemplary life in various aspects. And yet, didn't Triumvirate also fall short? Many evil deeds had been carried out and accomplished using Triumvirate's Sacred Tradition as a deadly weapon. *I don't know that I can say that belief in Krystos is the only way, Most High.* Frederick's anxiety strengthened as no specific metaphysical translation came, leaving the words "only way to salvation" relentlessly twisting away at his soul. Seconds turned too quickly into a minute, and still no justification came to the rescue. *What can I do, Most High?*

"Frederick, what is your answer?" whispered the Elder, interrupting Frederick's internal machination. "It is a simple question, with either a yes or no answer."

"I want to be quite sure of my answer," replied Frederick, glancing over at the Truth Seeker. He lapsed again into thought, afraid. His heart sank as he realized that there was no way out, no escape. The 77th commander braced himself, and spoke the truth, at least the truth as he knew it:

"Believing in and following Krystos, who paid with his life, so that we may live reconciled with the Most High is the Way."

"But is it the ONLY Way? Do all other ways fall short?"

"I don't know."

"Yes or no, Frederick."

"I don't know, Elder. I know that Krystos is *the* Way, but I do not know if He, and Triumvirate, is the ONLY way, the only true spiritual path to the Most High."

"Yes or no, Frederick."

"With all due respect, Elder, you have asked me to be completely honest, to tell the whole truth in the Test. And 'I don't know' is honestly what I believe, at least at this time. A 'yes' or a 'no' would be a lie."

"Frederick, *I don't know* is not an acceptable answer. You must answer yes, or no."

The words struck at the core of Frederick's soul. *I'm doomed!* The terrible feeling of failure washed through him—there was no way out. *My Wing—the 77th, no, Most High, they fail if I fail. They shouldn't suffer for my defect . . . "*

"Frederick, the choice is simple, and you must choose now." The Elder smiled, but the grin exuded no warmth, no friendship, no support. It was a challenge, a dare. The 77th Commander looked back at the Elder, took a deep, slow breath, and made the only choice available.

"My choice is to resign from Triumvirate, effective immediately."

"W-what? You can't resign, not now, not in the middle of the Call."

"There's no prohibition preventing a resignation—that is a time-honored tradition of Triumvirate once one is past his or her mandatory service commitment, which I am. I invoke my Most High-given free will, and resign now, this very minute. The Truth-Seeker can attest to my honest and firm intention." Both Elders looked at the Truth-Seeker, who nodded affirmatively.

"I still don't know that I can accept this, Frederick."

"Please, honored Elders, you asked me to choose, and I did. I could not answer your question with a yes or no answer. The 77th's judgment must not depend upon my success—or failure."

Right then, a strange, yet nonetheless vaguely familiar feeling welled up inside of Frederick, throbbing warmth that pulsed throughout his body. Frederick watched the two Elders, Recorder and Truth Seeker draw back, staring, mouths open in a state of shock, anger, and fear.

"What is it? What's wrong?" cried Frederick. Out of the corner of his eye he saw his wings, but not the normal white color. No, a slight shimmering, glowing aura of white radiated forth, and as he looked down at his breast, it too exuded a transparent glow of wondrous, yet unwelcome light.

"He is being possessed by the Evil One!" exclaimed the lead Elder, and, turning to the Recorder, said, "Call the warrior gull-hawks, and bring the squad here immediately!"

Frederick stood helplessly, his being iridescent, his body pulsating. A new sensation washed over and through him, a feeling of love, deep, total love and acceptance of himself and the gull-hawks in front of him. It was the most amazing feeling! But why now—here, when he had found a way out, not a great solution, but at least one which was best for the 77th?

"Oh Most High!" cried Frederick. "What do you want from me?"

"It is not the Most High, it is the Evil One, Frederick," said the Elder, Patrick—as he, the other Elder and the Truth Seeker backed slowly away from Frederick.

"No it isn't, Elder. I am being filled with an—it's hard to describe—almost heavenly feeling of love and grace. It cannot be from the Evil One. Forgive me, Elder, but you are mistaken."

"No, Frederick, it is *you* who are mistaken. You are mistaken about your faith; your inability to speak the correct answer just now—that Krystos it the ONLY true path to salvation—has brought the inner truth out about you. And that inner truth is—you are an agent of the Evil One. Our judgment over you in regards to the Call may be clouded due to your questionable resignation, but possession by the Evil One is grounds for excommunication, so either way, you will be out of the Flock. And if I have my way, put to death!"

"No, you're wrong, you're wrong, Elder! I feel, truly feel the Most High's love and presence, it's Him, there is no way this is evil!" urged Frederick. Before he could say anything else, the Recorder gull-hawk returned with not one, but three squads of Warrior Gull-hawks. The Recorder pointed at Frederick, who was immediately surrounded by one of the squads, while the other two surrounded the Elders, the Recorder and the Truth Seeker.

"Take him to the place of Isolation, and keep him well guarded. He is an agent of the Evil One." The Elder ignored Frederick's ongoing pleas, and spoke firmly to the squad leader, who turned and relayed it quickly to his squad. Frederick was desperate now, his body out of control, the intense, wondrous feeling of the Most High's presence grudgingly giving ground to a new sensation, a strong, foreboding sense of despair and loss.

"Fly with us, commander, but do not veer from our flight pattern," said the squad leader, his tone clearly lacking any respect for a gull-hawk who quite recently held a much higher rank. The squad leader was in command now, a great charge given to him. He would bring in the agent of Evil; there would be no escape. He gave a formation order to his squad, and they lifted off, with Frederick prodded along with them, pliant and defenseless.

With dusk falling, the fourteen gull-hawks were an eerie group, with thirteen gull-hawks surrounding a flickering, bright gull-hawk-like flying creature. Any who might have witnessed the scene would have wondered what the strange light was emanating from the middle of the squad. The two Elders, the Recorder and Truth Seeker flew directly to the Apostle's cove to report what happened. Two important events had occurred; first, a surprise resignation in lieu of a probable failure of the Test, very, very rare for a gull-hawk who had attained the rank of Commander. Second, and more telling, was the unquestionable indication of evil right in the midst of the sacred Testing Beach. In the very midst! The Apostle would be quite concerned, and quite relieved that the cancer had been identified. The two Elders were elated—the Call had succeeded beyond their wildest hopes!

Frederick, however, was the opposite of elated. He flew mechanically, downcast, his mind muddled, his heart broken despite the sensation of oneness with the Most High. *I'm ruined. How could this have happened? What is this incredible feeling of love, and did it come from the Most High, or the Evil One? What will happen to me? I've failed the Call! Oh Most High, what have you done? What have I done?* All these thoughts jumbled through Frederick as he struggled to stay up with the escort squad.

He was led to a large cave above Home Beach, several hundred yards from the shore, back in a stand of tall cedars. The squad landed outside the cave's imposing mouth and walked inside, Frederick still in the middle, following obediently. Despite the growing darkness, Frederick could make out elite warrior gull-hawks throughout the inner cavern, guarding the outside of what appeared to be smaller openings carved into the sides of the main cave. The squad leader spoke to the gull-hawk in charge, who led the entire contingent to a small cave located at the very back of the main cavern.

"In here," said the leader, motioning to Frederick, who had to crouch to enter the tiny opening, and as he did so, he glimpsed two gull-hawks posted as guards behind him. He stumbled into the little cave, enveloped by blackness with a sliver of gray from the opening barely visible. Frederick heard a rumble, felt the ground move, and then the gray opening vanished—everything turned black. All except his body, which still emitted a faint glow, but even that was fading, fading along with the immersion—but now distant feeling—of unconditional love.

Too soon, all that remained was despair, and total, monumental failure. He had resigned his command—a crushing disappointment—and from Triumvirate. But worse, he stood accused of being possessed, an agent of the Evil One. That meant Frederick will have lost—in addition to his rank—his standing in the Flock, and with that, his chance for love with Olivia. What was left to live for?

Chapter Seven

On another beach, many miles to the south, met another gull-hawk council.

In this council, however, the discussion centered on events more lofty—and certainly more important—than the fate of one miniscule gull-hawk. *This* council discussed and debated sacred territory, divine right, and the will of the Almighty—Almighty El-Rah—at least as they perceived the will of the Creator of the Universe.

"It is time, my brothers. The Song of El-Rah—blessed be his name—states that we are to reclaim the sacred island after the fourth full moon following the alignment of the four great sky lights. We need to act now in order to fulfill Shahadah's destiny!"

"Abdullah, your interpretation of the Song is a bit—ah—aggressive. I'm concerned about killing gull-hawks in order to regain the island. I don't want the blood of thousands of gull-hawks marking our glorious day. And, the Song says nothing about massive bloodshed, at least not in the verse you are referring to!"

"Nothing is said about death and dying, you are right, Malibakr my brother. And yet there is no proclamation against slaughtering infidels, either. We've often had to impart El-Rah's will with the liberation of souls. Why should this time be any different? Do you expect Triumvirate to just *leave* if we ask *nicely*? They consider the island sacred, too. No, my brother, we will have to *prove* that we are ready to fulfill our destiny, that our Flock is stronger, that our way is truer. I want to know what our great general has to say about *how* we are to reclaim the island. But be clear—I say it is time to end the treaty where each of us shares the island. I am tired of this sharing, this so-called joint ownership—two cannot own the Sacred Island, only one, and I believe it is ours! What say you, Calid?"

The general surveyed the other five gull-hawks gathered in the council of the Rashidun. Abdullah, Ali, Malibakr, Umar and Hassan were all loyal, faithful, powerful gull-hawks who Calid knew could be counted on in the upcoming struggle. Each had a large, devoted following, although some of those respective followers were not always congenial.

But in the Rashidun, only recently resurrected after many generations, the various factions had come together, and had reconciled in a way that Calid could only describe as miraculous. Surely El-Rah was guiding the diverse followers of Shahadah, and surely he would lead them to victory. No, it would not be easy, and lives would indeed be lost. Although he felt the heartache of loss . . . his elder brother was killed in battle many years ago—he knew that El-Rah honored all followers of Shahadah who died for His cause by bringing them immediately to the heavenly Paradise. And the lives of others, whether infidels or rebels, well, who could say what plans the El-Rah had, perhaps eternal life in hellfire? His fellow Rashidun members awaited his word, so he began:

"First, let us remember that our Sacred Song tells us— 'Nothing will befall us except what El-Rah—blessed be his name—has ordained. He is our Guardian. In El-Rah

145

the faithful put their trust.' My brothers, I have utmost confidence in our warriors and the ability of my officers to lead them. I have utmost confidence in our faith, and our courage. I have utmost confidence in the support of all Shahadah gull-hawks. And, I have *more* than utmost confidence in El-Rah; I have complete and total belief. I say we take the island before the next full moon. I am not as learned about the Song of El-Rah. What I am learned about is defending the SouthLand and advancing the Shahadah faith. We can win a great victory, and we should not shrink away from our destiny!"

The others looked at him, somewhat awed by his strength, commanding nature, and purity of faith. And yet despite this awe, Calid did not have the final word. No, the Council of the Rashidun always needed to hear from Malibakr. While Calid was the military leader, and the group turned to Abdullah for passion and zeal, it was Malibakr who the Rashidun looked to for leadership, spiritual insight, and the final blessing. According to the Shahadah Tradition all gull-hawks were equal spiritually, with no hierarchical command structure like Triumvirate. And yet Shahadah gull-hawks—like all gull-hawks—some excelled at certain disciplines, some at others. Malibakr had demonstrated a unique ability to perceive the spiritual truth out of the midst of competing factions, to find clarity in uncertainty, bring calm in chaos.

Malibakr surveyed the other five, still a bit unclear about how to proceed, or what to say, in order to guide this group that in turn must lead the Shahadah flock. With a deep breath, he took the only possible path.

"Let us pray for guidance first, my brothers, let us submit our will to El-Rah's will to ensure we are aligned with His wishes, and able to truly follow His commands." Malibakr marked his prayer place with his sharp talons, making the required diamond shape, and faced the sacred balanced stone, which stood only a short flight away. He prayed:

"El-Rah is great! El-Rah is great! I testify that there is no god but El-Rah, and that our Prophet is the last and truest messenger of El-Rah, who brought us the great message of salvation. Glory be to Thee, El-Rah, and blessed be Thy name and exalted Thy majesty. There is no deity to be worshiped but Thee. We seek your protection against our accursed Enemy. We seek Your eternal guidance. Let us be silent and hear Your words."

Malibakr began the ritual, time-honored bowing and bending, bringing his small head down to touch the ground. All six performed this ancient ritual of submission to El-Rah simultaneously, five times in succession. Upon the last touching of their heads to the sand, they remained in that position for several minutes, staying silent, submissive. When the prescribed time was up, the six straightened up in unison, saying once more:

"El-Rah is great! El-Rah is great! There is no god but El-Rah!"

Malibakr took a deep breath, eyeing each of his Shahadah brothers. "I have listened to, and repeated in my mind over and over, the passages from our Sacred Song which could guide us—must guide us—in this endeavor. I believe that we should indeed act, and I'll tell you why. All of the right pieces are in place: first, the song never mentions that we should share our Sacred Island with others; therefore, that holy ground must be returned to our wings, not to share, but to possess for the Almighty.

147

If we wait to take back what is rightfully ours, then we could be judged as remiss, undeserving! Second, we have the great general, Calid, who now commands the greatest military force seen by the Flock of Shahadah. And third, the Rashidun has been re-formed, and for the first time in many, many, many generations, our various clans have reunited. We have put aside our petty squabbles and are now more powerful than we have ever been, not just militarily, but more importantly, spiritually. Until we got together, prayed together, and proclaimed El-Rah's greatness together, the time was not ripe for conquest. Now it is—everything is in place!

"But don't for a moment become overconfident, that our victory will be easy. Although we have El-Rah on our side, the Triumvirate flock also believes it has El-Rah—who they mistakenly call the Most High—on its side as well, and will fight for the island with determination, power, courage, and zeal. It saddens me to think of the bloodshed that will flow, my brothers. I wish we could have obtained the island through diplomacy and peaceful persuasion, but clearly that will never occur, as long as Triumvirate claims it as their holy center. And it saddens me because the beliefs of two faiths are not so far apart. I wish in my heart of hearts that Triumvirate gull-hawks could just accept our Prophet and the Song as the final word of God, and we could live in peace."

"But they have not accepted," interrupted Abdullah, "And they continue to proclaim their faith to be the *only* way, and have for seventy generations since the Prophet revealed the true way! Let us show them which faith is actually true on the battlefield. El-Rah will decide, for El-Rah is great!"

The other gull-hawks joined in the chant, and it echoed loudly across the craggy, limestone ledge. After several minutes of passionate worship, they quieted down, and began to plot their takeover of the island, and for inflicting a serious blow to the Triumvirate flock, those misguided followers and defenders of Krystos.

Frederick woke with a start, badly disoriented in the surrounding blackness. He had been dreaming about the Test of True Flight, about being swept away by a sudden squall at the end of the Test. Lightning flashed around him, getting closer and closer, when he felt a thundering strike; the corresponding jolt tumbled him out of the sky, falling down towards the angry sea. He struggled for control, but the winds were too strong, and he braced for impact. Abruptly, he awoke! Groggy at first, the events of the previous day came rushing back, bringing the gull-hawk's mood back into dark despair, a perfect reflection of his prison, the dark, black cave.

He remembered it all—the inability to answer that last, impossible question, his resignation to save the Wing, light shimmering around and through him, and the curse from the Elders. He had failed, failed the all-important Call of Confidence! Frederick could not fight the sinking feeling. He had done nothing wrong, had told the truth—so why was he here?

Of course, my truth wasn't the "right" truth, the Triumvirate truth. That was clear, but not the shimmering light and exquisite feeling of unconditional love that enveloped me after I made the terrible choice to quit. Was it the Evil one, the enemy, as the others had said? How could that be? No—it was such a huge presence, so accepting and understanding, like coming home to your home and family after a long journey, only better, much better!

Despite what the others said, Frederick was not convinced, in fact he believed, wanted to believe, could not otherwise believe, that what had washed through him was the Most High, and the others were being deceived or misled by their own limited faith.

"But all of this speculation doesn't matter, because here I am, in isolation, and in big, big trouble," said the gull-hawk to himself. Frederick realized he was talking out loud, but decided that the sound of his voice improved the gloomy, black silence. "I wonder how my Wing is doing," he continued, "do they know about me? Did they pass? Who'll take over? Gregory, of course, he's as capable as I, a strong leader, and the gull-hawks respect him. And Nathan—he knows how to work with the gull-hawks' spirits. Together, Gregory and Nathan will be able to handle the 77th, even though they'll be shaken up. But they should have passed, and the resulting blessed relief, and the celebration of survival, should mitigate their loss of me as 77th Commander."

He continued his one-way conversation in the dark cave: "But what am I to do? What will happen to me?" More questions poured out, and he eventually shook his head, exasperated at his pointless speculating. Eventually, exhausted and frustrated by the lack of answers, Frederick remembered his training, and began the process of stilling his mind. *Peace, be still, and know the Most High* he whispered, breathing slowly, turning his breath in and out. Between the pitch black and absence of sound, Frederick found a deep, calming meditation.

Later, the stone rolled away, a small salmon flew in, and the rock rolled back. Not a word had passed; Frederick knew that the guard probably knew little about what was to happen to him. He gratefully ate the salmon, drank from a small pool of water in the back of the cave, and went back to his meditation. He fought down surges of panic, and claustrophobia. He cast about inside his soul for the Most High—outside, too, wherever the Creator might be. *Where are you? What do You want from me? You did this, made my wings turn to light, so help me, Most High!* The cave yielded no answers, and nothing came from within. Frederick sat patiently, breathing steadily, alone, waiting.

The twelve Elders gathered at the High Council chambers, the Apostle and his trusted, personal recorder already present. Just outside the chambers a squadron of elite warrior gull-hawks stood, vigilant as always, with added tension—this was a very special meeting, well outside of the usual routine. Olivia took her place among the twelve, and they were immediately informed that there were only two agenda items, first, the problematic Shahadah activity near the Island of Eternal Peace and second, Frederick. The Apostle led them in prayer, and then opened the meeting.

"Item one: the Island of Eternal Peace Wing commanders are reporting increased and unusual activity of Shahadah gull-hawks around our most sacred island, much more than come for normal Shahadah pilgrimages. That activity includes a sharp increase in the number of patrols of Shahadah warrior gull-hawks. It could be nothing—possibly just battle exercises, but it was enough to warrant these reports, and to inform the High Council directly.

"Item two: most of you know that every gull-hawk of the 77th Wing had passed the Call except Wing Commander Frederick. Frederick was on the way to passing—which would mean that the entire Wing would—when he hesitated on the final question. The Elders pressed him for an answer, but he kept saying that he did not know the answer to that question—is belief in Krystos the only path to salvation? The Elders testing demanded a yes or no answer, to choose one or the other. Most unexpectedly, Frederick abruptly resigned from Triumvirate!

"What?"

"Impossible."

"What was he thinking?"

"That gull-hawk is trouble."

The Apostle held up his wing, cutting off the Council's outburst. "According to Elder Patrick, who presided as judge, Frederick resigned so that his inability to answer the question would not cause the entire Wing to fail."

The Apostle looked around the Council, his eyes sweeping past Olivia, who sat in stunned silence. *Resigned? I can't believe it! Why couldn't he answer that question? Did he sacrifice himself for this Wing? In his failure, did he triumph?* Her thoughts swirled in an instant, but were cut-off with the Apostle's next revelation.

"A resignation from Triumvirate would not normally be sufficient reason to convene a special High Council session; however, what happened right after Frederick resigned has me most concerned. As you will hear from Elder Patrick and Cornwallis, it may be that Frederick was temporarily possessed by the Evil One!"

Olivia gasped, and her heart sank. *Control yourself! No matter what, stay calm, see what comes about.*

Fortunately for the female Elder, the Apostle's last statement had launched another firestorm of protests, accusations and pleas to the Most High. The Apostle raised his voice, commanding the Council to obey the rules of silence. When order had been restored, he once again spoke in his quiet, authoritative voice.

"I believe these two events are intertwined, that the Evil one is once again active in our land—more so than normal—and influencing gull-hawks in devious ways. In my prayers, the guidance which came pointed out that these next few months will be crucial in Triumvirate history, that the balance of power could swing away from good—to evil—depending upon our actions, and of course, the grace of the Most High."

Jeremiah, arguably the most compassionate High Council Elder, asked: "In Frederick's strange occurrence, why do you suspect possession by the Evil One, Apostle? Olivia felt relief with the question. She had wanted to ask it, but was afraid to voice her concern—and by chance expose her feelings for Frederick.

"It was the Evil One, I am sure of it." The Apostle turned to see who had interrupted. It was Patrick, the Elder who had been questioning Frederick.

"Yes, there is no question in my mind," said Cornwallis, the other Elder present at Frederick's failure.

"Elders Patrick and Cornwallis were Frederick's inquisitors, and have arrived at their own conclusions," replied the Apostle, irritated by another breach of Council protocol. He nodded to the two, acknowledging their part in witnessing the extraordinary event. "Nonetheless, it is impossible to know with complete certainty what truly happened. I've asked this question myself several times in the last few hours, and Jeremiah, I'm glad you've asked it as well. The Recorder and Truthseeker present during Frederick's Test of True Faith are each waiting outside. We'll have the Recorder recount the events *as they actually happened*. Patrick and Cornwallis, hold your comments until after the Recorder is finished. Then, and only then, I want you each to add your interpretations—*and just those!* No accusations, please. The Truthseeker will be available for questions as well, in addition to verifying the accuracy of the Recorder's witness."

The Recorder was called in, followed by the Truthseeker. The first gull-hawk quickly recounted to the High Council the events of Frederick's Test of True Faith. Trained in observation since first flight, Recorders could be counted on to be completely objective, especially when paired with a Truthseeker. The Council sat quietly, transfixed by the accounting—the only movement came from Patrick and Cornwallis nodding.

Olivia watched the two as they sat there, the two zealots practically gloating. *How they love to see others fall—Patrick thrives on it!*

The Recorder finished, the Truth Seeker testified to the veracity of the telling, and Patrick added a few bits from his perspective, not contributing much, but clearly enjoying the attention. Olivia chafed at the un-Krystos-like antics of Patrick and Cornwallis, especially since they were profiting at another gull-hawk's possible demise and outwardly exhibiting uncompassionate behavior.

The Apostle could see it, too. He put up his wings up, calling for attention. "Elders, please remember the serious matters that have brought us here this evening. This is not a time for personal gain. In fact, let us recall that being on this Council is not for self-advancement; it is to serve, just as the original disciples called by Krystos served him, and his cause, and the Flock, and the Way. Recall Krystos's words *he who is first, shall be last*. And, assuming the Evil one is active, he may try to influence us—each of you—as well. So be vigilant, and keep your mind and heart centered on the Son, and the Most High!"

The Elders looked at one another and were taken aback, slightly ashamed and embarrassed, at least outwardly. Inwardly, several discounted the Apostle's words. While they wanted to serve, they were also on the High Council for control, and for power.

"Now you have heard the Recorder's recounting of what happened with Wing Commander Frederick. And, you have heard from Patrick and Cornwallis, who were present and witnessed what happened. I am going to retire now to the Apostle's inner chamber. My prayers will be intense, seeking the Most High, thirsty for Krystos's guidance. I suggest you do the same. Look deep within yourself—you must ensure the highest amount of clarity, and the least amount of self. The decision that I make, with your counsel, will affect not only one gull-hawk's life, but perhaps the entire Flock."

Each gull-hawk went his or her separate way as the Council meeting adjourned. All except Olivia, who hung back.

"Apostle, may I have a word with you?" She looked down, afraid of what she needed to say, but what must be said.

"Yes, Olivia, what is it? What's wrong?"

"You . . . you may know I met Frederick several years ago. I felt then, and had a similar feeling after several encounters, that Frederick and I shared a special connection. I've not had much opportunity to explore what exactly that connection is. Now, it doesn't really matter, except I think I could bring insight to the Council by paying a visit to Frederick. Find out what is going on with him right *now*, and do my best to ascertain any evil presence. I'm not exactly sure what should be done, but I do feel strong inclination to go and see him—but only with your official approval, of course."

"I sensed some discomfort from you, Olivia. With the source revealed, I am relieved it is this 'feeling' that is the cause. Additional insight would be most valuable. While I am confident that unusual energy is present, I cannot in all honesty say that the Evil One is or was in possession of Frederick—although it is a distinct, real possibility. You have my authorization, Olivia, to go on my—and your— behalf. Find out from Frederick what was going on during the last minutes of the Call. And, Olivia, you must be fully alert, mindful, and stand with a true and pure heart. Leave immediately if you sense evil! And report first thing to me in the morning."

A disturbing thought came to Olivia as she flew to away. *Was Grandmother Grace right? Wasn't this what she said would happen? Not every detail, but something like this? Most High, how can that be? What is truly going on?*

Olivia made her way to the prison cave, and presented herself to the Captain of the Guard. Recognizing her and the authority of her Council position, the Captain quickly escorted her to Frederick's cell. The warrior gull-hawks rolled away the stone, and she peered inside the dark cavern. It was hard to make out the outline of a gull-hawk in the middle of the musty cave. "Frederick," said the Captain sternly, "You have a visitor, a very important visitor—Olivia of the High Council. You are to answer all of her questions truthfully. If you make any attempt to escape or harm her, the four warrior gull-hawks stationed here will put you down, without mercy." The Captain turned to Olivia and motioned her in. "If he makes a threatening move, just yell."

"Thank you, Captain, but I think I can handle Frederick. Still, I appreciate your caution just the same. Please excuse us for a few minutes as I interrogate our prisoner."

Frederick sat, momentarily stunned. He finally mustered up something: "You, Olivia, Elder Olivia. What are you doing here? You should be distancing yourself far, far away after what's happened. And now you're here—and you want to interrogate me?" Olivia looked back sadly. She shook her head, and blinked back tears.

"Oh, Frederick, I am truly sorry to be together with you in this terrible situation. Please know that I have come—with the Apostle's permission—to ask you what exactly happened at the end of your Test of True Faith. Frederick, most of the High Council believes you to be under the spell of the Evil One. Are you?"

"No Olivia, I'm not, well, at least I don't think so. I don't sense any evil presence. Sadness, intense disappointment and bitter failure, but no evil."

"You look beat down," she said softly. "Tell me exactly what transpired. And Frederick, you do realize how serious the charges are against you, don't you?"

Frederick stared through the dim light at Olivia, so close, just a few feet away, but a vast chasm separated them. He choked back a sob, unwilling to show Olivia his pain.

"I've replayed the events a dozen times, dozens. I attempted to answer the final question as truthfully as I could, you know, the one that asks 'is belief in Krystos the only way to the Most High?' I've struggled with the word *only* for some time now. I *know* it is a *true* flight path, a true way, but how do I know with one hundred percent certainty that belief in Krystos is the one and only way? I don't. So, my answer was 'I don't know,' and that was the absolute truth for me, Olivia!" Frederick looked intently into Olivia's eyes, hoping that she understood. He took a deep breath, and then let it out.

"My answer was not going to be correct, no question about it, but I could not let my Wing fail because of me—that would not be right. So I resigned my commission.

"As I spoke my answer to the last question, a feeling from deep in my soul came forth, penetrating what seemed like every cell of my body. This feeling—it's hard to describe it—was more than just a mere sensation. I don't know—the best words I can use is *total love* for everything—all creation—mixed with overwhelming joy and a true sense of 'rightness.' Olivia, I felt and even 'heard' what I believe to be the Most High. And, in none of these experiences have I felt anything that approaches what we think of as evil."

Olivia shook her head. "It's hard for me to believe you couldn't answer the final question in the correct way, and even harder for me to believe you resigned from Triumvirate. It's shocking, disappointing, maddening all rolled up together. I know I don't really know you, but your belief about Krystos not being *the way* is a complete surprise to me."

"No, Olivia, I'm not saying that Krystos is not *the* way, just that belief in Krystos as the only son of the Most High may not be the *ONLY* spiritual path to salvation and enlightenment."

"Frederick, what do you say about Triumvirate's teaching that the Evil One is very seductive and often masquerades as the Most High so that he can lead gull-hawks astray?"

"I am very aware of that, which is why I can't be totally sure that I was in the presence of the Most High. I doubt, however, that the Evil One could generate that much love. The incredible love that I experienced can only come from the Most High, through Krystos!"

Olivia frowned. "But what about the last question? Why couldn't you answer it with a 'yes?' It is the fundamental question that, in the end, defines your belief and whether you are in Triumvirate and our Flock, or not! What you say contradicts the teachings of Triumvirate, Frederick. How long have you had this idea? I hate to say it, but I can see now why Apostle wanted the Call of Confidence."

"How much time do you have here?" Frederick chuckled softly as he shook his head. "I knew about the question coming in, and thought about it plenty. Olivia, when it came down to answering that question in my heart of hearts, I could not say that I knew for sure our way is the only way. A *true* way to the Most High, absolutely, and perhaps the best way, but the *only* way? No, I cannot say that for certain."

"What about Krystos's own words that 'no one can be with the Most High except through Krystos himself? What could be plainer than that?"

"Yes, those words are in our Sacred Traditions, and integral to the Triumvirate creed. However, they just don't ring true for me, Olivia. Quite frankly, I highly doubt that Krystos ever spoke them. Of all the witnesses to Krystos's words, only one has Krystos 'saying' those particular words. If that were the absolute key to Krystos's message, the most critical phrase, wouldn't *all* the witnesses report it—again and again? One phrase, by just one witness several generations after the fact and that is the most important belief of all?"

Frederick stared at Olivia, his eyes intense but pleading. "Look, you and I have not had enough time together to discuss our deepest thoughts, or even talk about our lives. Olivia, a long time ago I met someone from the Shahadah faith, and I saved his life in a terrible storm." Frederick recounted the story of his time with Malibakr's family. He finished the story:

"I left Malibakr and his family with the belief that their Way is in all likelihood a valid path to the Most High. That seed of doubt—or truth—was planted then, years ago. So when the question came, Olivia, I could not lie. The Truthseeker was there! The easy thing to do would have been to say our way is the only way, but it was not the truth, and we swore to tell the truth."

The High Council Elder shook her head. "Oh, Frederick, with that belief and what happened afterwards, I'm afraid that you'll be expelled from the Flock. While I appreciate what you did for the 77th, resigning so that they could pass, your other actions are too . . . "

"Did the 77th pass?" Frederick interrupted Olivia, urgency returning to his voice.

"Oh, I'm sorry—you're cut off in this cave. Yes, the 77th did pass. There were some on the Council who didn't want to accept your resignation, and advocated for failing the whole 77th, but our traditions are clear, and they were overruled."

"Thank the Most High, that's what I needed to hear." Frederick nodded slowly, exhaling a long, slow breath. Olivia studied him carefully, alert for anything unusual.

"Yes, the 77th is back in good standing with Triumvirate. You, however, are in trouble. It'll be difficult for the other Elders, or myself for that matter, to allow you to remain in the Flock. We're in a tough spot."

"Most High, Most High," Frederick sighed, exhaling deeply. "That has been my greatest fear in the past few hours, Olivia. My career is over, my life is ruined! And I didn't ask for any of this." He shook his head. "My friend Joram did say that something powerful would come out of the Call, something that could shake up Triumvirate."

"Joram, who? Tell me about this Joram."

"He's a friend that lives near me, an old gull-hawk who himself was asked to leave Triumvirate many years ago. But I never thought I would follow him to this particular end."

"Then you are talking about the exiled former Elder and Wing Commander gull-hawk. Frederick, you've been spending time with him? Really? He is trouble! Well, at least now I know where some of your ideas have come from. Why did you get mixed up with him? If the Council hears about your association with him, you are doomed for sure!"

"He wasn't excommunicated. Joram said that he was still part of the Flock, although not welcome in most places. Olivia, I was aware that befriending Joram could be a problem, but to be honest I would rather spend time with him and his wife Dayleen than any of the Elders or the Apostle—except you, of course. His ideas resonate with a deep, true part of my soul. Just like my visit with Malibakr, where I saw for myself what that "foreign" faith can be when practiced with compassion and truth. But my ideas about whether Triumvirate is the *only* way were derived much more from the rescue of Malibakr than my conversations with Joram and Dayleen. Please understand that."

"Frederick, I feel so sorry for you. I know you meant well in all of this, but with your last revelation about Joram, there is little question that Patrick and Cornwallis will call for your excommunication from the Flock. And although the Apostle has stayed impartial—as is his duty—in the end he probably won't oppose it, either. And that means that I will not be able to see you again!"

Olivia hid her head behind her wings, unwilling to let Frederick see her tears. Frederick approached gingerly, and put a wing out. Not backing away, Olivia nestled up to Frederick. Her body trembled, and Frederick found his love pouring out to her, enveloping her, trying with all his heart to comfort her. Olivia accepted his affection for a few long moments, then slowly pulled away.

"We don't know each other well, but despite that, I think I love you, Frederick. And I wish, how I wish the circumstances were somehow, some way different. But they're not! I will do what I can in the Council to soften their hearts. In the end, I fear the worst will occur. For what happened, you will be put on trial. Nothing can stop that." She stopped, and they looked at one another in the semi-darkness. Olivia spoke again, her voice a low whisper.

"But no matter what happens, know that even if there comes a time when you are all alone and it seems as if no one cares, there is someone who does care, me! I've got to go now, and I will report what I've learned here to the Apostle. Of the Elders, he is the most levelheaded about this and will not submit to hysteria, or zealous prosecution. Good-bye, Frederick, good-bye . . . "

And with that tender farewell Olivia retreated from the cave. Frederick wondered if those would be the last words he would hear her speak. He heard the stone rolling back in front of the cave opening, and the darkness swallowed him again. Alone in his thoughts once more, Frederick pondered his chances. Pretty bad, he mused, and then soberly realized what excommunication meant. *No sanctioned rituals, prayers, or anything connected to Triumvirate. Outlaw, shunned, a friend of no one, except other outlaws, heretics and low life's. Well, Joram, are you happy? You were right about all of this, and even though your friendship may have sealed my fate, I would not do anything different—how could I? Otherwise I would've been living a lie, hiding from the truth. Somehow, I know that Krystos is in charge, and that the Most High will prevail.* Frederick began an uneasy meditation, a centering prayer, clinging to the hope that something good would come of all of this.

As Frederick prayed, Olivia flew a long, circuitous route back to her sleeping place. A combination of resignation and grief dominated her soul. She wanted time to think, but the thought patterns from her visit with Frederick fired in a dozen different directions, possibilities and scenarios. Starting with Frederick's recounting of the incident at the Call, his failure due to not believing that Krystos was the only way and the resignation to save his Wing. Olivia marveled at Frederick's ingenious self-sacrifice, even when his own future was lost.

163

But that good thought evaporated as she remembered the double taint of his encounter with the Shahadah, and clandestine friendship with the exiled Joram. How much trouble was Frederick in, exactly? Where did the ex-77th Wing Commander's loyalty lie, deep in his heart? Was Frederick a threat to Triumvirate? *I didn't sense any malice or evil or treason from Frederick. But as High Council Elder, it is my sworn duty, my sacred calling to protect and preserve Triumvirate. Krystos, my savior, if ever I needed your guidance, your wisdom, it is now!*

As she prepared for sleep, Olivia said her prayers, asking with all her soul for guidance and insight into what seemed like an insurmountable problem. Her last thoughts before sleep were of Frederick's tender, loving embrace.

Heavy, cool fog shrouded Home Beach, with only a small promise of sun to come. After saying morning prayers, Olivia flew to the eating cove reserved for the Apostle and Council Elders. Olivia did not see the Triumvirate leader so instead scrounged around for a few small fish and shrimp. Afterwards she flew straight for the Apostle's rock formation. She spied the Apostle inside his protected ledge and banked a sharp turn towards him after he motioned for her to land. Olivia began to talk, but the Apostle waved her off.

"Before you tell me about Frederick, the most recent scouting reports from the Island of Eternal Peace have grown worse. More Shahadah are present—a lot more. I have increased our own patrols in response and heightened our overall alert status. Olivia, I am greatly troubled by all of this; it was much better when each of the Shahadah clans were fighting among themselves. Now they're united, are much more dangerous, and I think willing to break the Island peace treaty. Not good, not good at all. Pray with me, Olivia, pray for the Most High's wisdom, first about Frederick, and then about this deteriorating situation at our beloved, sacred Island."

The Apostle looked to the sky and raised his wings in supplication. "Oh, Most High, Creator of all, hear our prayer . . ."

Afterwards, the two sat in silence. The moments of quiet helped restore Olivia to a centered, calm place, a much-welcomed change after the angst of the last two days. After a bit, the Apostle motioned to Olivia to begin her report.

"Well, my visit with Frederick was both illuminating and mystifying. As expected, his mood was down, quite somber and subdued. Apparently, the strange, faint glow which Patrick and Cornwallis witnessed has occurred to him a couple of times before, and it is often accompanied by a soft, inner voice, which Frederick strongly believes is the Most High, or perhaps Krystos. He's not really sure. In regards to that which triggered the event—his failure to affirm the *exclusivity* of our faith to save—Frederick insists that while our way is absolutely true, he cannot swear that others are not, and in the presence of the Truthseeker, could not, did not want to lie, even though the wrong answer would mean failure. And so he resigned, resigned to give his Wing a chance at success. Frederick was most interested about the 77th's fate. He had not heard how they had fared, and was genuinely overjoyed to hear that they had passed."

"Did you learn anything about how he has come to doubt the unique, exclusive saving power of the Son as the only true path to God?"

"Yes, and it isn't good," Olivia admitted, and then shared Frederick's story of his encounter with Malibakr, and budding friendship with Joram.

The Apostle took a deep breath, shaking his head slowly. "You don't mean ex-council member, exiled and near outlaw—you do, don't you? Krystos! I've heard rumors of such! Yes, Olivia, that bodes bad, very bad indeed. We should have excommunicated that rogue, heretical gull-hawk and put him to a painful death! No, forgive me, Olivia, that's too harsh. But look, once again Joram is causing trouble for Triumvirate. You think that Frederick was influenced by him?"

"I don't know much about Joram, Apostle." She looked intently at the Triumvirate leader, a realization flashing through her mind. *This anger towards Joram—it's personal!* Olivia filed away her insight and, treading carefully, asked: "Is it true that you two served on the Council at the same time, years ago?"

"It is." The Apostle's short, firm answer ended that line of questioning. "Please Olivia, tell me more about your visit with Frederick."

"Frederick said that he valued his friendship with Joram, and in some ways Joram was a teacher to Frederick."

The Apostle was silent, but his face mirrored anger, exasperation, and sadness. "Oh, Joram, why do you haunt me still, after all of these years? You see, Olivia, Joram was a powerful Elder, combining a deep faith, strong charisma with love and a wry sense of humor. He and I were competitive in everything, and quite frankly it was this competition that helped bring me to the pinnacle of Triumvirate. Joram was in line for the Apostleship as well, but his inability—or unwillingness—to crack down on heresy and his ultimate defense of alternative, sometimes contradictory ideas led to his downfall. Like Frederick, he could not fully believe our Sacred Scripture! He revealed this secret only to me, so concerned was he of excommunication. But one belief he could not keep quiet was the one that as it turned out was the final straw to his being expelled. And that belief was his claim that we gull-hawks had evolved from simpler forms of life, in direct conflict with our Scripture. In addition, he believed gull-hawks have the potential to evolve further, so that all gull-hawks could become like Krystos. Those beliefs, with his public advocating of them, brought him into direct conflict with all that Triumvirate flew for. He was officially pronounced a heretic, forced off the High Council, and into permanent exile."And now he returns to my life, our lives, in the form of Frederick, his apparent protégé. I think about Joram from time to time, Olivia, and I miss his exuberant spirit. But I can't tolerate Frederick's questioning of our faith, especially with this conflict with the Shahadah reigniting. We must deal with Frederick swiftly—and decisively—so that we can close ranks and focus on a potential defense of our sacred island."

"Is there any hope for Frederick? Truly, I don't sense that he is evil or bad, just misguided. Apostle—do our Sacred Traditions have any flexibility?"

"Olivia, our rules are clear—extended contact with an exiled member of Triumvirate is grounds for suspension and/or possible expulsion. Unfortunately, when combined with the failure at the Call and the odd occurrences of light—the High Council really has no choice."

The Apostle paused, taking a deep breath. "We must bring Frederick up on charges of heresy *and* fraternizing with an exiled Triumvirate member. The Council will have to decide whether Frederick is exiled for a set period of time, expelled permanently, or, and it could come to this, Olivia, excommunicated. May the Most High have mercy on his soul if the evidence is as damning as it appears."

"Apostle, it sounds like there is no hope for Frederick."

"Hope? Yes, there is always hope—if we turn our lives—our heart, soul, mind and spirit—over completely to the Most High. I'm not sure that Frederick is willing to do that, however. For now, we need to reassemble the Council. Thank you, Olivia–your input was invaluable."

Olivia felt her heart sink. Her visit with Frederick was supposed to help the situation, but the report she had given—especially about Joram—seemed to have turned the Apostle's mind against Frederick.

When the full council met, the result came quick and unanimous: Frederick must stand trial—any doubt evaporated after twin disclosures of contact with Shahadah years ago and Joram most recently.

As was the custom, the Apostle would act as judge, two council members would prosecute, two would defend, and the other eight act as jury. Truthseekers would be present to ensure accuracy and Recorders would track the proceedings. Olivia volunteered for the defense team, joined by Jeremiah. Not surprisingly, Elders Patrick and Cornwallis asked to prosecute. In her heart, Olivia knew that only a miracle would keep Frederick from exile, and excommunication loomed a real possibility. Still, she hoped for the best, as it truly seemed that Frederick had no evil in him. But as the High Council adjourned, Olivia remembered another of Grandmother Grace's premonitions: 'involves some kind of trial, with a member of Triumvirate being questioned about his faith.' *Most High, her premonition was right on. How can that be?* Olivia made up her mind right then to get back to Grandmother Grace's cave as soon as was possible. In the meantime, however, she had worked to do, with Jeremiah.

The two High Council Elders wasted no time and flew immediately to the Prisoner's cave. They asked the former Wing Commander more questions, trying to formulate a defense. Frederick rejected the 'I didn't know that Joram was exiled' defense as untrue. The three talked well into the night, discussing strategies, trying to anticipate how Patrick and Cornwallis would attack Frederick. All three agreed that with the evidence available they'd much rather be prosecuting! At the end, a consensus emerged around the only available approach: admit to what had happened, emphasize Frederick's outstanding record and loyalty to Triumvirate, and ask for a merciful sentence, preferably a short, solitary suspension. Frederick would ask to be reassigned to the Reserve Force, and submit himself to refresher courses in Triumvirate theology. It was the best they could hope for, and the two High Council Elders left the cave feeling a bit hopeful, although still apprehensive, Olivia especially.

Alone again, Frederick worked hard to quiet his mind as it raced from scenario to scenario, possibility to possibility. After the initial struggle, he found a rhythm of breathing that brought him a time of relative calm. Much later, he opened his eyes, feeling somewhat restored, even in the dark, lightless cave.

Frederick reflected on his fate—the upcoming trial, the probability of suspension, as well as the chance of excommunication. Even though Joram seemed to be fine with living under that stain, Frederick was not. To be thrown out of the Flock which he loved and had served for most of his life was terrible, almost like death itself.

Despite his belief that other ways were valid, Frederick still loved Triumvirate, and Krystos. Sure, he disagreed on certain key points of doctrine, but despite that, he still belonged to the Flock—would die for it if necessary. And what about Olivia? If he were excommunicated, he would never see her again. No, it was better to take a few lumps here, suffer a suspension, and even an inglorious demotion rather than lose his identity and the opportunity—even improbable—to love Olivia. As he drifted off into a restless sleep, the future looked mostly bleak, with only a tiny speck of hope in vast universe of darkness.

The next morning dawned foggy and cool, although Frederick had no idea of this since he remained isolated in the dark cave. Awakened by the rolling stone, Frederick was led out by a complement of thirteen warrior gull-hawks, an entire squadron. The brightness of the day, even with the blanket of gray fog, blinded the young gull-hawk and he stumbled momentarily. One of his escorts started to prod him, but the squad leader quickly assessed the full situation, halted the procession and allowed Frederick a chance to orient himself and let his eyes adapt. After a minute Frederick signaled his vision had returned, and the squad leader gave the command to fly. Frederick knew that he could probably escape from these gull-hawks, even though they were part of the elite Apostle guard. He was a formidable flyer, after all, one of the best! But, escape would be the same as admitting guilt, which was not really an option, and Frederick was determined to see this through. What could the Elders really prove? No, he needed to face the entire High Council, including the Apostle, and hope his defense would be enough to soften the blow. He flew on with the squad, flew crisply despite his lack of flight—or moving much at all—over the past two days.

Too soon the formation arrived at the Council's Beach and the adjacent Apostle's Rock. Looking about, Frederick noticed significant activity, much more than what the trial of one measly gull-hawk should require. *Something else is amiss! What could be going on?* The landing of the squad cut off his speculation, and he was bustled across picturesque Council Beach, protected by tide-smoothed rocks and short cliffs, a beautiful cove on any other day but today.

As he came through the entrance, the severity of the situation hit him like a cold blast of winter's wind. There was no traditional welcoming ceremony, of course. No, this was a trial—no smiling faces; just stern, silent gazes all around. The Apostle sat on his rock, the prosecution Elders to his right, and Olivia and Jeremiah on the left. The remaining High Council Elders, who along with Apostle would determine innocence or guilt, stood a bit further off to the Apostle's right, while on the Apostle's far left sat several Recorder and Truthseeker gull-hawks. Surrounding the beach area were numerous squadrons of warrior gull-hawks, patrolling in tight patterns. Frederick was led to Olivia and Jeremiah, and the escort squadron withdrew to the rear, guarding the entrance into the cove, but with eyes glued to the former Wing Commander.

After all were gathered and silent, the Apostle opened the trial with a standard call to order, followed with a prayer:

"Oh Most High, hear our plea . . .
Be with us today as we judge a fellow gull-hawk.
Help us to present the evidence fairly, both for and
    against.
May all of our words be truthful, in accordance to
    Your standards.
For You are our Judge of all Judges,
And we feel Your presence in our midst, right now."
Amen."

"This trial has been called by the High Council of Triumvirate," continued the Apostle without pause, "of which I am the head. Frederick Gull-hawk, you are charged with three crimes: the first is heresy; the second possession by the Evil One, and the third is fraternizing with a permanently exiled Triumvirate member. Our trial rules are simple: The prosecution presents the evidence, the defense answers, the prosecution rebuts and summarizes, and the defense answers and summarizes. The Truthseekers are here to ensure that the truth is told, and the Recorders are here to not only remember the trial for history but also recount any events that they may have witnessed. Is that clear?" No one moved, although the atmosphere crackled with intensity. "Elder Patrick, please proceed with the Triumvirate's case."

Patrick launched into the case against Frederick with his usual zeal. He began by laying out what had led up to the Call, the rumors of unusual events and questionable teachings. He followed with a detailed recounting of Frederick's failure to answer the final question of the Test of True Faith, along the unexpected—and totally inappropriate in Patrick's opinion—resignation. Next, he spat out how Frederick shimmered with light immediately after the failed Test. He then recounted Frederick's own contention that the Shahadah faith was valid. And finally, Patrick pointed out Frederick's damning admission that he had spent a number of occasions with Joram, an exiled Triumvirate gull-hawk. Patrick concluded his prosecution with a powerful condemnation:

"The failure to affirm Triumvirate's fundamental credo, that 'the only way to the Most High was through the Son as illuminated by Triumvirate' combined with his belief that the Shahadah faith was 'true' clearly denoted heresy in the highest degree! Add to that Frederick's own admission to spending time with the exiled—and off limits—Joram, so that charge was proved as well. Guilt is not a question, High Council, and witnesses are available if the defense attempts to refute any of the charges." Glaring at Frederick he sat down, then nodded toward the Apostle, finished.

Jeremiah spoke first for the defense, quickly and fully admitting to all five points presented by the prosecution. However, Jeremiah asserted that the appropriate conclusions drawn from those events were not those stated by Patrick. To begin with, Jeremiah argued, the unusual events and questionable teachings led to the Call of Confidence. Thus, there was a "punishment," and certainly serious consequences, already for these acts. Frederick's 77th Wing performed brilliantly in the Call, and all except Frederick passed both Tests with near-perfect scores, and Frederick was on his way until the final question hesitation and subsequent resignation.

"No other Wing had done so well; surely their Wing Commander had something to do with this outstanding performance," asserted the High Council Elder. "Yes, Frederick did seem to be unable to answer the final question, and therefore would have failed the Call, except for his unexpected resignation. But that resignation—while sealing his own fate—allowed his Wing to successfully pass the Call. That selfless act cannot be dismissed as lightly, and with apparent contempt, by the Prosecution."

"Apostle, I object to the defense's final statement."

"What *exactly* is your objection, Patrick?"

"The defense is making Frederick out to be some kind of saint with all this talk of selflessness. We have no evidence of his true motive. For all we know, this all could be part of the Evil One's plan."

"Patrick, you objection is recorded, but overruled nonetheless. Let's stick to the charges at hand, please. Jeremiah, you may continue."

Jeremiah nodded toward the Apostle. "Frederick not only gave up his command, but his membership in Triumvirate, and status in the Flock. These are great losses, immense sacrifices. What more shall we extract from him? Additional punishment for his failure, and the unexplained possession, would be neither just nor fair."

Jeremiah looked slowly around the High Council, momentarily holding the gaze of each Elder. "Remember, please, Frederick's outstanding war record and unswerving loyalty to Triumvirate. This gull-hawk is—was—one of our very best. I ask that Frederick be sentenced to one moon cycle in isolation, be required to take remedial courses in theology, and submit to examination at the end of each moon cycle for an entire year. At that point, he would be subject to full evaluation, and the High Council would determine a new course of action. This is Frederick's first offense. We ask first for mercy and second for a fair, honest judgment for the former 77th Wing Commander."

Patrick stood immediately, his eyes flaring at the defense's brilliant mea culpa strategy. Seeking to regain the momentum, he launched into his closing with a call for justice.

"True justice must be served by the trial, and mercy left to Krystos," affirmed the prosecuting Elder, reiterating the overwhelming evidence against Frederick and then brought forth his clinching point—extended contact with Joram is potentially an offense which carries excommunication as the most extreme punishment. Patrick finished strong:

"Under these circumstances, excommunication should be, must be the consequence—and the proper justice—given these heretical, forbidden behaviors." Satisfied, he sat down and exchanged a smug glance with Cornwallis, both of them nodding at the righteousness of their case.

Olivia began the defense's closing by reminding the court that excommunication was not a mandatory consequence of fraternization with Joram, the exiled—and generally off-limits former High Council Elder. No, all the facts and circumstances needed to be considered for true justice. Olivia yielded to Jeremiah, who recounted Frederick's record with Triumvirate, his heroics in battle, his reputation as a promising Wing Commander, and his lack of prior brushes with heresy—or any past misdeeds or blemishes on his record. Before the Call, Frederick was what Triumvirate sought in all their warriors.

"But the Call brought out Frederick's weaknesses, and exposed several errors," continued Jeremiah, his voice quiet, conciliatory. "The defendant expects punishment, as he did violate the rules. However, excommunication is too harsh for this battle-proven veteran, this former Wing Commander."

Jeremiah looked toward Olivia, who took over the final defense closing: "Look at the results of the Call for 77th—except for Frederick's individual Test of True Faith—their individual flying was superb, the Wing performed as a whole admirably in the Test of True Flight, and there were no other signs of heresy among the other one hundred sixty-one gull-hawks of the 77th. These outstanding gull-hawks were well prepared. And who led them?" Olivia again looked around at the Elders. "Frederick was their leader! 'We are known by our fruits,' it is said in the Sacred Scriptures. So what does the 77th's performance tell us about Frederick?"

Olivia ended her argument, "We plead guilty to the charges, but with extenuating circumstances. Justice must be done, but it must be tempered with mercy. Triumvirate was founded on both fundamentals. I don't have to tell you that as Krystos flew among us, the Son of the Most High *forgave our transgressions*, and told us to *sin no more*. Frederick admits his transgressions and accepts that he must be pay for his actions. The now ex-Wing Commander also asks for forgiveness, and will do his best to sin no more, at least within the limitations of being a gull-hawk, by the grace of Krystos."

With both sides complete, the Apostle dismissed the remaining eight Elders to discuss the case and render their verdict. Frederick sat with Olivia and Jeremiah, concerned about the trial, and also fretting about some of what was said. *I understand how they don't want gull-hawks to talk with exiles, but still, Joram is a great gull-hawk, wise, compassionate, deeply spiritual, and an outstanding flyer. To expel someone like*

Joram is a sign that something is wrong with Triumvirate. He didn't fit in, his beliefs didn't all jibe with Triumvirate's, and he was removed. Not good for Joram, not good for me! A sinking feeling began to grow in Frederick's stomach and stayed there for the next hour, waiting, watching, and waiting some more. Another hour and still no Elders. The Apostle let everyone take a lunch break and then back to more nerve twisting waiting.

It took until the sun was nearly down before the eight Elders returned, apparently with a decision, or so their stern faces said.

"Elders, you have reached your verdict?"

"We have, Apostle. We find the defendant, Frederick Gull-hawk, guilty of the charges of minor heresy and fraternizing with an exiled, former member of Triumvirate."

Even though Frederick was expecting this, the sour feeling in his stomach worsened, both from the judgment and in anticipation about would come next.

"And the punishment you recommend/"

"We were persuaded by the defense's argument. Frederick has paid—and will pay—a steep price for his error. He does have an outstanding record with Triumvirate. His Wing did perform well, and they all passed. Only Frederick came close to failure, and his resignation nullified that, uh, potential."

"We, therefore recommend, one year of an exile of solitude, Apostle. However, at the end of exile, Frederick's admission back into Triumvirate as a member in good standing will depend upon him being able to answer the final question of the Call in an uncompromising, affirmative manner. If he cannot, then his exile will be extended one year. At the end of each year Frederick will have the opportunity to rejoin by swearing to our creed. Until he can do so, it is our belief that he should not be a part of the body of Triumvirate."

"An excellent sentence. I don't believe I could have come up with a more appropriate punishment myself. Truly, I sense the Most High's mercy and Krystos's wisdom in your recommendation. Thank you, Elders and Recorders and Truthseekers." Turning to Frederick, the Apostle said, "The exile will be carried out on islands on our northwest boundary. You will be escorted there, and there you must stay, with no contact with any Triumvirate gull-hawks. Frederick, do you understand your sentence?"

"I do."

"Before your exile, our tradition allows you to make a final statement. Do you have anything to say to the High Council?

"Yes I do, Apostle." Frederick felt a nudge from Olivia, but brushed it off, whispering that he needed to say something for the official record. "I love the Flock, Triumvirate, the Most High, Krystos, and the 77th. I apologize for my actions. In my heart of hearts, I don't believe I have done anything *seriously* wrong. Nonetheless, I do see the need for punishment for breaking our rules. Quite frankly, I don't understand these mystical events. They are beyond me and my control. Above all, honored Apostle and High Council of respected Elders, please, please let no stain fall on the 77th. They are innocent of my errors and inability to pass the Call. Those gull-hawks are true to Triumvirate and above reproach . . .

Frederick looked down, and in that instance felt a familiar, but disconcerting feeling. *Not now!* The young gull-hawk felt his body pulse with unconditional love, and could see the beginnings of a faint glow. He felt, or heard, a thought arise within and whisper, *"Frederick, your trials are not over. Trust in me. You have much work to do."* The inner whisper faded, leaving Frederick alone, in the middle of the cove, the Elders glaring at him, his being still encompassed by the strange white light, and unconditional love.

"See, he is possessed. I told you so!" pronounced Elder Patrick.

"The Evil One is here—quick, call for our elite warriors," exclaimed another Elder.

"Oh Most High, save us!" cried a third.

"Quiet!!" shouted the Apostle, taking over the potentially chaotic situation. He turned to former Wing Commander and demanded, "What's happening to you, Frederick?"

"I'm not entirely sure, Apostle, like I just said, I don't have control over these occurrences! What I do know is that I was overcome with a powerful, loving presence. And I 'heard'—or felt a voice within—soft, almost an impulse, but it somehow translated into words."

"What did the voice say?"

"That my trials and work are not over, that I need to trust the Most High."

"Apostle, how can you stand and listen to him?" This time it was Elder Cornwallis standing, and pointing an accusatory wing at Frederick. "He is clearly possessed, and should be—must be—excommunicated and banished from the Flock."

"Elders, I remind each of you of the requirement of order and procedure in this trial. A judgment has been reached and punishment set. When Frederick's exile is over, if these 'occurrences' continue, then we'll deal with them!" He turned again to Frederick, and was about to say something when it happened again. Frederick felt the powerful force well up inside him and the light pulse with more intensity. This time, though, the voice that had whispered within now chose to *speak through him*. Frederick stood paralyzed in front of everyone, his voice controlled by something, a presence definitely not gull-hawk.

"Be mindful of your judgments, Triumvirate Elders. Your one hundred generation tradition is strong, but imperfect. It contains error, and if it is to grow and thrive as one of My Ways, it must evolve, be improved and perfected by those alive. For has it not been spoken, that I am Most High of the living, not of the dead?"

The voice abruptly ceased, Frederick collapsed, and the surrounding gull-hawks sat speechless, shocked. The squadrons of warrior gull-hawks who had been patrolling landed immediately, concerned with the strange proceedings. "Are you all right?" one of the squadron leaders asked the Apostle. His question broke the silence, but before he was able to answer, Patrick and Cornwallis found their own voice.

"He is indeed possessed, speaking such blasphemous heresy. How dare he question our Sacred Traditions? Exile is not enough, neither is excommunication; Frederick, or whoever he is, must die!!"

"Yes, death to the demon gull-hawk!" exclaimed another Elder. "Quick, before he grows stronger!"

Several others of the Council joined in, while a few, like Olivia and Jeremiah, remained silent, momentarily stunned. Did they just hear the voice of the Most High? What they heard was disturbing, very disturbing. In the midst of the cacophony, the Apostle asked for, then demanded order! The beach grew silent, and the gull-hawks waited to hear what the Apostle might say, hoping he would bring much needed certainty and calmness. The Triumvirate leader looked directly at Frederick, his face stern, but his eyes sad, regretful.

"Frederick, what just happened has changed my mind as to your sentence and punishment. I'm sorry, truly sorry, but what I just witnessed with my own eyes and heard with my own ears proves to me that you are dangerous, extremely dangerous. What emanated from your mouth is heresy in the worst, and traitorous to our Flock. You have called for, in as many words, claimed to be, or be speaking for, the Most High or the Son. No longer are you a gull-hawk struggling with his faith, but instead one pretending to be a deity, which we all know is the highest blasphemy. You've left me with no choice, Frederick." He shook his head, and took a long, deep breath. "As Apostle, I have the power to order excommunication—if at least two-thirds of the High Council agree."

He turned away from Frederick and faced the High Council. "I am now asking for such a vote, since it is my judgment that this gull-hawk presents a clear, imminent danger to our faith and must be excised from the body of Triumvirate. How many of you agree?"

The Apostle looked around the beach, and ten of the Elders agreed. Only Jeremiah and Olivia did not vote yes; each abstained, and that saved his life, for a unanimous vote of the Council would have elicited the death sentence. Frederick, still languishing in a semi-state of stupor, could only stare at Olivia, the Apostle, and the other Elders as they sentenced him to a terrible fate, not death, although some said it was a fate worse than death. Excommunicated! His soul cast out and eternally damned. He glanced towards Olivia, but her eyes gave no warmth, no real recognition of what was—or had been—between them. She was in High Council Elder mode, loyal to Triumvirate, allegiance squarely with the Apostle. He shuddered inwardly, but any other feelings were cut off by the Apostle.

"Then it is agreed; Recorder, you have noted the voting, that it was done properly with more than enough votes. The excommunication of Frederick Gull-hawk is effective today, the 3rd day after the new moon, and the eighth moon of the year. Frederick will be escorted to the borders of our Flock, and never return, upon pain of death. Contact with him is forbidden; any who do come across him accidentally will turn immediately and fly away, otherwise risk excommunication themselves. Warrior escort gull-hawks, please take the prisoner to the northwest border. Your escort will be in silence. When you reach the edge of our territory, where the land turns to ocean, turn back. Frederick, you are to fly on, and may the Most High have mercy on your possessed and misguided soul."

Frederick was immediately surrounded by the same escort gull-hawks who brought him to trial. They walked him off of the Council's beach in a fast pace. Frederick barely had time to look towards Olivia one last time before being hustled off the beach, in flight, headed west.

The excommunication had occurred so suddenly, without warning, that Frederick was airborne before the full reality of the moment hit him, but it did strike, and the blow hit hard. Only his many hours of training kept him in the air, for emotionally and mentally he was devastated. The escort flew through the night and well into the next day, stopping only briefly to feed and to drink. When they reached the ocean, the escort immediately turned back, leaving Frederick in the air, alone, utterly spent.

He had been taken north of his former home, but Frederick was pretty sure where he was, at least physically. Spying a tall, beautiful grand fir on the peninsula, Frederick flapped to it and landed on an upper branch. Exhausted to the core, he decided to spend the night there, and in the morning—well, part of him hoped that morning would never come, for what was there left? An impressive sunset out to the west unfolded unnoticed by Frederick, who before always stopped to admire the Creator's handiwork. A sunset meant nothing now, as his worst fears had come true, he had lost his command, his love, and his life in Triumvirate.

He sat on that branch for a long while, through the coming of dusk and into the onset of darkness. The night seemed devoid of life, of energy, and it mirrored his spirit— empty. He was tired—tired of battling, tired of struggling to find and know the truth. But one thing did beckon, one call rang out strong, and that was the need for water. He was suddenly, powerfully thirsty! He cocked his head, and discerned a nearby watercourse, close by, off to the south. A thin but waxing moon provided sufficient light, and soon he stood on a large, flat stone in the middle of the river, gulping the watery, life-giving cool sustenance. The moon reflected off the slow moving current, sparkling and dancing all around.

The water and light interplay reminded Frederick of the morning of the Call, awakening to the dream of Olivia, the hope for their love, and future together. He closed his eyes, listening to the river upstream dropping over a series of short, winding falls, providing a soothing cadence.

Thinking about where he had come from, and where he was now, he felt empty, with no future possibilities. Emptiness all around, everywhere.

But still the moon danced off the river, and the young gull-hawked looked closer at the light—there was something unusual about it, something not quite right. He leaned over, looking keenly at the river, and saw his own reflection in the flowing water. Compassion welled up, emerged from the emptiness inside—appreciation for the gull-hawk in the water, a gull-hawk who had brought the 77th through the Call of Confidence, successfully, but at a price. One had to be sacrificed—Wing Commander Frederick—now gazing back, compassion and empathy emanating from the reflection's eyes, and filling the empty vessel of his spirit.

He continued to stare into the water, caught in a hypnotic-like trance, mystified by his own image, eyes full of sadness and love and—something more. Hopelessness and despair had drained away, were gone, replaced by compassion, which was transforming second by second into a deep, universal acceptance. Warmth and kindness was looking back, and acceptance, true acceptance of who he was, a gull-hawk with great strengths, a few glaring weaknesses, good traits, bad habits—a work in progress, striving to bring forth the gifts he had been given.

And the reflection was changing too, changing as the all-encompassing soulful love rose throughout his body. Frederick did not fight the feeling this time, the familiar pulsing, a seemingly miraculous outflow of blissful love and spiritual energy. He saw his reflection begin to glow, radiate light, not brightly, but steadily, rising and falling with his breath.

Gratefulness filled his heart, and strength coursed through his wings. *Most High, I've not lost you!* The young gull-hawk continued breathing, watching as the light grew brighter with the inflow and dimmer with the outflow. Over and over, in and out, Frederick stood in that place, enveloped by the loving acceptance of his Creator.

All, apparently, was not lost.

Keep reading for an early look at:

After the Messiah Had Gone

Book II: The Quest

Coming Summer 2016

Chapter One

The most sacred place in either NorthLand or SouthLand was, without question, the Island of Eternal Peace. Paradoxically, that made the Island the site of the most conflict in either land, and over which the most blood was spilled, and most selfishness perpetuated.

The Island of Eternal Peace lay just below the southwest border of the Triumvirate Flock's territory, and just above the northwest border of the Shahadah Flock's territory.

It rose abruptly in the middle of a deep, wide, windy strait—known simply as the Great Strait—which served as the natural boundary between the two flocks and their two island-continents. An abundant population of very old, very lush, deciduous trees interspersed between tall, thick evergreen stands grew on this small, but fertile isle. On the west side, basalt cliffs commanded sweeping views toward the vast ocean. There were long swaths of the Northland and Southland shorelines, respectively owned by the two flocks. On the east side of the treasured island a rocky, magna-built mountain rose sharply over a thousand feet; flat ledges near the top afforded outstanding vistas over the island and both territories north and south. Gull-hawks at either of these locations enjoyed panoramic views without having to expend any flapping energy.

Despite these two prominent features, it was the pure, clear, fresh water lake carved in the middle of the island that drew each and every gull-hawk pilgrim. All felt compelled to stop, reflect, and wash his or her body—and spirit—in the bluest of blue lakes. This water, this rare jewel, was for both Flocks, for both faiths, the most sacred part of this most sacred island, the holiest of holies.

Back to the beginning of recorded time the Island of Eternal Peace has played a central, essential role. In fact, the holy island and the sacred lake were central to both Shahadah and Triumvirate ancient creation stories.

In the beginning, the Most High was alone. Although He—the gender the Most High has almost always been referred to—was complete in His aloneness, one day He decided to create a physical universe. And so out of His very being He brought forth rays of light, and then sound. The light and the sound came forth in a most powerful explosion, sweeping out in all directions, and as it receded from the Most High, became tangible essence—known commonly as matter. On the second day He created from this matter the Sun, this special planet, and the rest of the heavenly bodies. The next day, the Most High created on His chosen planet water and land and air and fire, and on the fourth day He organized these into great islands, oceans, rivers & seas, air to breathe, and fire deep underground to keep the planet warm and growing. The following day He created the winds and clouds and rain and snow and ice and storms and lightning. On the sixth day He created all of the living things that grew from the dirt, walked the ground, or lived in the water. And on the final day of creation, the seventh day, He created beings that flew— majestic—and clearly the Almighty's favorite.

It is said that after the Most High had finished creating the flying creatures, but before the gull-hawk had been created, He saw a tiny island on the Earth, and fixated on it, and the small,

burgeoning volcano that grew in its middle. He smote the vol-
cano, pushing it downward and filled it with water. The water
mixing with the hot volcano created a wonderful steam, and the
Most High delighted in the warm mist, the rising vapor. From
this delight the Most High decided to form one more creature,
a flying thing that was primarily white—like the clouds being
formed by the misty steam. And so he created this bird, a pow-
erful flyer that could live anywhere on the planet, not too big,
not too small, not too fast, not too slow, strong yet graceful—a
perfect blend of all birds, the gull-hawk.

After He had finished, the Most High looked upon His cre-
ation, and said: "This planet, this world is a good thing. From
I it was created, and although I am finished for now, creation is
not complete. That which I have created will continue to grow
and evolve and change, for I will set it in motion with My own
divine spark, and I will monitor its progress, from My vantage
point here in the heavenly realm, and also from within all that I
have created."

And with those words the Most High sent forth a portion
of His spirit and it entered all of the planet's matter and mol-
ecules and atoms, so that there was no place that He was not
present. And inside the gull-hawk he placed an extra dosage of
Himself: intelligence and curiosity and compassion. Once this
was accomplished, the Most High rested, and meditated on His
accomplishment, His creation, and what was to come.

Both Shahadah and Triumvirate gull-hawks taught a
version of this story of creation as part of the tradition of
the Creator—know as the Most High to Triumvirate and
El-Rah by the Shahadah. And both knew that the island,
which the Most High had fixated on so very long ago in
the creation of the gull-hawk was claimed to be the Island
of Eternal Peace—once again the center of the brewing

conflict. But while the two Flocks shared a similar creation story—along with several other overlapping sacred traditions, the faiths practiced by each were distinctly different. Each flock believed without doubt their faith was the only true path to the Most High.

And the Island of Eternal Peace had once again become the focal point of the very old battle for supremacy of faith.

As a rule, gull-hawks avoided night flying, venturing forth only if lost, escaping extreme weather . . . or desperate. Triumvirate's patrols were no exception, despite the recent increase in Shahadah warrior gull-hawks activity around the Island of Eternal Peace. Several generations ago a peace treaty had been crafted—following yet another war— between the two enemies which awarded each flock their own, respective place where warrior gull-hawks could be stationed on the island. Both flocks received locations on the west cliffs and the eastern peak although neither could place warrior gull-hawks near the Island's sacred lake, which was deemed off-limits to all but worshiping gull-hawk pilgrims.

Triumvirate kept two Wings on the west cliffs and two on the eastern mountain while an identical number of Shahadah gull-hawks were also in place, ever vigilant, always wary. With the increased presence of Shahadah warrior gull-hawks flying around the island, the Triumvirate wings had doubled their watch from dusk to dawn. The 12th Wing was stationed at the highest level of the eastern mountain—the critical link in the Triumvirate sentry system. Just as Frederick was settling into his exiled sleeping place far to the north, Stanley, Commander of the 12th

Wing, walked toward one of his most trusted squad leaders. Jerome Richards felt anxious but concealed it—he greeted his commander warmly, smartly.

"Evening, Commander. What can I do for you?"

"Just making the rounds, Jerome. I want the gull-hawks to know that *I know* and see the commitment they are making. What's your assessment of the readiness of your and the other squads?"

"Well, sir, the 12th Wing warrior gull-hawks are definitely ready if the Shahadah gull-hawks try something, anything. Our gull-hawks feel that the Most High is protecting us. We are not the aggressors here—after all, we're protecting holy ground!"

"Agreed, the Most High is with us, Jerome. We will need His blessing, power and vigilance if we have to fight. You know that the Shahadah gull-hawks are fearless, and they believe just as strongly that the Most High—El-rah is their name—sides with them." Stanley let out a long exhale, then looked back at Jerome.

"Our generals believe that a night assault is unlikely . . . Shahadah gull-hawks have never attacked in the dark before, so our night-time heightened state of awareness may be overkill. Nonetheless, we must not let our guard down! Are the gull-hawks clear about that?"

"Yes, sir!"

Stanley nodded to Jerome and moved on to make contact with the other squad leaders on watch. Finally satisfied, he flew back to his command perch and settled down for a light sleep . . . he would be no good as a leader if he were not fresh. He knew the gull-hawks under his command, as well as the other Wing stationed here would defend the Island with fierce determination and utmost courage. He also knew that there were thirty Wings within a day's flight who could help in case of an attack, and had just been put on high alert. In addition, Stanley had requested reinforcements—twenty Wings—from the High Council to offset the increase in Shahadah gull-hawks, but they were still at least a day away, depending upon how seriously the Elders had taken his request. Stanley prayed to the Most High that no attack would occur before the reinforcements arrived. He was confident the Triumvirate reinforced defenses could . . . and would repel an invasion from the Shahadah gull-hawks on the Island, even when combined with the additional Shahadah gull-hawks seen in the vicinity. But a large force of Shahadah warrior gull-hawks could be trouble. "Krystos speed to you," he whispered to the twenty Wings. He sighed, and closed his eyes in preparation of sleep.

Many miles from Stanley's perch an unusual noise filled a large, yet remote beach. The sound of thousands of gull-hawks landing in the dark, with only a quarter moon to shed light on the suddenly busy stretch of flat sand. A vast multitude of Shahadah elite warrior gull-hawks were assembling at this secret staging area, not all that far from the Island of Eternal Peace. Stanley and the other Triumvirate commanders were absolutely correct about *past* Shahadah behavior when it came to night fighting . . . it had not occurred in many, many generations.

However, the potential retaking of the sacred Island and the fulfillment of ancient prophecy provided an incredibly rare opportunity, requiring new methods to be employed. The great Shahadah general Calid flew to a prominent rock and addressed the assembly—his glorious troops, and his chosen path to immortality.

"EL-RAH IS GREAT! EL-RAH IS GREAT! THERE IS NO GOD BUT EL-RAH!"

The elite Shahadah gull-hawks echoed their general with loud cries ringing up and down the crowded beach. The General, fearing discovery from the cumulative roar, quieted his troops with a brief gesture. These warriors possessed incredible discipline, following instructions without fail, including those that would bring loss of life. None feared sacrifice! The General turned towards Hassan perched close by, who led the gull-hawks in a short prayer:

> "In the name of El-Rah, the Compassionate, the
>   Merciful
> All praise belongs to El-Rah,
> Lord of all worlds
> The Compassionate, the Merciful,
> Ruler of All Days, and the final, Judgment Day
> Show us the straight way,
> The righteous way, the harmonious way,
> the honorable way
> The way of those You have graced,
> Not of those who wander astray."

Calid allowed the words of the one true God sink deeply into the gull-hawk warriors. Then, he spoke, his voice passionate:

"Our flock—Shahadah—is poised to accomplish something that for most of us, and our fathers, and their fathers and their fathers, and for our mothers and their mothers and their mothers, for many, many generations in fact, to accomplish something that has been only a dream, just a quiet squawk of possibility. But now, prophecy can be fulfilled. Each of you, whether you live or you die tomorrow morning, will be remembered forever. Before the next sunset, we take back what is rightfully ours, which rightfully belongs to El-Rah, blessed be his name!!!"

"EL-RAH IS GREAT! EL-RAH IS GREAT!"

Malibakr flapped next to Calid, and embraced his general. Malibakr surveyed the impressive gathering crowding the long beach. He raised his wings, and the Shahadah faithful rose in a tremendous, appreciative roar for their beloved Malibakr. He slowly lowered his wings, and the disciplined Shahadah warriors hushed immediately.

"You, warriors of El-Rah, have been given our plan of attack, and each of you know your sacred role. But in the heat of the battle, when even the best plans go awry, you'll need to draw upon your faith and fearlessness to win. The enemy will also fight well—make no mistake about it—so be ready for an opponent who will not yield as long as a breath flows in their heathen bodies. So take that life, and trust El-Rah to judge them . . . as He so righteously will. There will be no lasting, final peace until the Island is ours, back in the hands of El-Rah, blessed be his name. Follow without fear our General Calid, and your battalion leaders, and individual coterie lieutenants. Go powerfully with El-Rah, and victory is ours!"

He motioned towards Calid—who nodded back to Malibakr—and general spoke again to the secret gathering: "You know the prophecy, Shahadah gull-hawks. Just as important, you have your unwavering faith, and you know the battle plan to take the Island. Never, ever forget that you make up what could be the finest warrior

196

gull-hawk force ever. We will be victorious; this is our righteous destiny."

"The enemy will be confused with our attack, thrown off balance, coming in the black of night. They won't know how to defend what they can't see! We, however, know exactly where they are and how to defeat, and how to destroy them. We will overwhelm the Triumvirate infidels and reclaim El-Rah's holy ground as our own. Tonight we fly by moonlight—and faith—to the secret beach a mere hour from the Sacred Island. You're ready for this—fly as you've practiced so many times before. We'll rest there briefly, then, we attack! Once victory is ours, El-Rah be willing, we will celebrate like no Flock has ever celebrated. Follow me, for El-Rah is Great, El-Rah is Great, there is no God but El-Rah!"

Calid flew off of the high rock, his gull-hawk escort directly behind. One by one, the Shahadah warrior gull-hawk battalions joined him, one hundred thirty gull-hawks in each, one hundred battalions in all. The thirteen thousand gull-hawk Shahadah fighting force looked terrifying as it flew off in formation in the partially moonlit sky. Silent except for the flapping of thousands of wings, they flew towards their staging area, the hidden beach within easy striking distance of the Island. Calid found a northerly air current and settled inside it; the wind would help them conserve precious energy.

Calid knew about the request for reinforcements from the Triumvirate gull-hawks on the Sacred Island, as his spy network was extensive. He had expected this but was not worried. Twenty Wings—what was another three thousand or so Triumvirate gull-hawks? They would be no match for his thirteen thousand gull-hawk force, especially since he already had three hundred gull-hawks on the island as part of the peacekeeping force. El-Rah is Great! They would be doing a different kind of peacekeeping once the takeover was complete. No, the battle for the Island would be over by the time Triumvirate's reinforcements arrived, and his remaining troops would be well positioned by then. And Calid had more troops poised for the next battle, another fifty thousand Shahadah gull-hawks, the largest ever assembled in recent memory! Take the island, then control the sky; his forces would do it, with the backing of El-Rah.

Calid pondered another bit of news from his spy network. Apparently, Triumvirate had excommunicated a Wing Commander gull hawk. Now this was a very rare occurrence. Several thoughts came to mind: He wondered what the gull-hawk must have done to deserve such a fate. Perhaps he should contact this gull-hawk . . . a former Triumvirate Wing Commander with a grudge toward Triumvirate could be a valuable ally in the war that will surely follow. Regardless, this strange turn of events had distracted Triumvirate from focusing too intently on the Island. *El-Rah is indeed great!* The General gave thanks again for the amazing way El-Rah worked in orchestrating this glorious, prophecy-fulfilling attack. He flew on, supremely armored in his faith, confident of ultimate victory.

The flight of the Shahadah warriors coincided with Frederick's nightmare. He was back in the Triumvirate prison cave, but the air had run out and he was suffocating. Olivia, standing outside the doorway, was unable to hear

Frederick's panicked cries. Or, she did not care. His cries grew fainter as he felt the life force drain away.

The gull-hawk awoke with a start, gasping for precious air!

For a moment Frederick was relieved that the nightmare was just a dream, but all too soon the awareness of his true reality rushed forward, and with it came immense sorrow, and despair. He had been stripped of rank and privilege and standing in both Triumvirate and the Flock. Olivia was off limits from him. He had lost so much, so very much.

Or had he?

The gull-hawk remembered the experience during the previous night, watching the river, and the clear message: *Most High, I've not lost you!*

It came back to him, the soul-filling love, deep sense of peace, and his reflection in the smooth water with the faint glow pulsing with each breath. He'd lost everything that seemed important, certainly everything that mattered in the world, the world of gull-hawks at least. But he had not lost his connection to the Most High, always precious, and now, of utmost, singular importance. It reminded him of one of his favorite sacred sayings:

Seek first the Kingdom.

At this moment, it rang so true—made total sense to Frederick, perfect sense. So what to do next? How exactly should he seek the kingdom of the Most High? The gull-hawk had no answers, and, still exhausted from the long ordeal, slipped back into sleep

The rising sun woke Frederick, the first sunrise he'd witnessed since the trial. He watched its patient, brilliant ascent. He whispered a morning prayer, then settled in for a long, needed meditation, moving quickly into a steady, rhythmic breathing. Thoughts flickered in and out, but Frederick let them go—there were still no answers within his own depressed ideas. It took awhile, maybe a long while, but eventually Frederick's mind became still, empty, clear. He continued on, letting his breath turn in and out, smooth, easy.

Frederick sat like this for a long time, high in the tree, absorbed in much needed communion. A thought finally penetrated his inner silence, bubbling up from the depths.

Focus.

He observed the sound of this word—foe-kuss—and then let it go, unwilling to grasp anything, unwilling to attach to any thought or word.

The word reappeared in his mind, *focus.* Although intrigued, Frederick was enjoying the calmness of the meditation more, and let the word slide away.

Soon the impulse, the whisper returned, stronger, urgent: *Focus!* The gull-hawk opened his eyes, took a deep breath, and asked, half in jest, "Okay, Most High, I hear you. I guess I need to *focus.* What exactly should I be focusing on?"

Frederick closed his eyes and waited. After all, he had nowhere to go, no one to see, no duties to attend to, no agenda to follow. He had finally received the "leave" he'd requested, only not exactly in the manner that he wanted.

But regardless, he was free.

Free.

The gull-hawk drew breath once more, turned it in and out, in and out. Another thought-impulse came through, this time several words, a familiar phrase, one that had come in the middle of the night: *Seek first the Kingdom.*

"Sound advice, Most High, or Krystos, or whoever or whatever you are. I hope I can follow it," said the former Wing Commander aloud. "Although, what else can I really do, after all?" His stomach rumbled loudly, and that decided his next step.

Frederick began to fly, suddenly quite hungry. By habit, he headed toward his typical feeding spot, one frequented by Triumvirate gull-hawks. Remembering his status, Frederick turned aside, but it was too late; he spied a pair of gull-hawks streaking for him. Coming up along side, one spoke:

"You are forbidden to eat here, Frederick. The High Council requests that you move away, far away preferably, for excommunicated gull-hawks are allowed no contact with gull-hawks of the NorthLand Flock. No contact, do you understand? No exceptions. We've been ordered to patrol this area and ensure the excommunication decree is strictly enforced. This is the first—and last—time we will speak to you. It would be best to find another home!"

They wheeled about and flew back to their patrol above the feeding area. Frederick wasn't allowed to explain, to tell them he had realized his error—he knew that he was not allowed to eat there and was turning around.

An outcast isn't listened to—he's cast out, after all.

The reality of leaving his home, never to return, however, was a sharp blow to the gut. As was the implied thought that High Council Elder Olivia wanted him to move away, too. He highly doubted she would want that, and the thought of losing her love hurt to the core.

Where to from here?

The gull-hawk thought about Joram and Dayleen, and scanned the surrounding area, flying in slow, rising circles with the help of a morning thermal, looking for his friends. A sobering thought came just then.

My only friends.

Frederick pulled out of the thermal and headed toward the ocean, remembering to *focus*. A soft tailwind accompanied Frederick as he winged his way down the rich, tree-choked valley in search for food . . . food that was not off-limits. If he flew out to the ocean, south of his old patrol area, he should find areas to eat that were mostly deserted. Perhaps there he could find some peace, and a meal.

Joram and Dayleen might be the only ones allowed to talk—or interact in any way—with him of all the gull-hawks whom he knew; as "exiles" they had little to fear from the threat of eternal excommunication.

Where could they be? At their island home? The volcano? *I hope they can make sense of this, find something positive, because as I see it right now the path ahead is full of heavy, dark clouds . . .*

When Frederick reached the great ocean he instinctively looked to the north, where several miles away rose StoneHeart Cliff. His patrol area, his command!

Was, that is.

Looking hard, he seemed to be able to pick out a squadron or two or gull-hawks. Frederick turned away, his stomach twisting in sorrow and deep loss. But from his place of pain a new thought, a pure, simple thought-phrase emerged.

Be here now.

This idea brought him back into the present, and just in time as a powerful gust forced the gull-hawk towards a rocky outcropping. Flapping mightily, he used the updraft to miss a nasty looking chunk of basalt by a mere wing span.

Thank you, Most High, for reminding me to stay present. While I appreciate the lesson, can we avoid another life or death situation for a little while?

He remembered the purity of *be here now* and felt better. Flying on, he reached a small, deserted bay that looked promising, teeming with fish and other prey. Frederick ate heartily, his ravenous appetite surprising.

The meal revived Frederick and propelled the gull-hawk toward the dormant volcano. Despite the admonition to stay focused on the present, his mind drifted back to his Wing—Gregory, Nathan, David. Were they still his friends? Maybe yes or maybe no, but it didn't matter since he couldn't talk to any of them, and they couldn't acknowledge him, so what was the use?

And Olivia, well, it was impossible for Frederick to imagine that there was some way, any realistic way back to her.

He had lost her.

The rippling effects of the excommunication expanded in Frederick's mind, draining off his former existence. But this time, with despair rising, Frederick remembered the pulsing light and fought back, yelling loudly,

"No! No!! No!!!"

His body shook, and he came close to falling out of flight, but the gull-hawk recovered and mentally stamped down the unwanted, unproductive feeling.

Focus. Be Here Now. Seek first the Kingdom.

That's all that mattered, that, and his friends Joram and Dayleen.

As he neared the diamond-shaped island at the bottom or the water-filled, dormant volcano, two gull-hawks flew out of the trees . . . as if from nowhere. Frederick dove to them—yes—it was his friends. There!

In a few moments, settled on the upper branches of a very old, very thick grand fir, the three stared at each other, each waiting for the other to speak. Frederick, bursting with emotion, began his story.

Acknowledgements

THE IDEA FOR this book sprouted thirty-five years ago, and the first true writing began in 1988. *After The Messiah Had Gone* has been a creative act for over half my life, and there are many people, places and events that deserve thanks, praise and gratefulness now that it is being brought to fruition. More than a labor of love, this story is an outpouring of my soul, has been my own personal "call" and quest, and an excellent crucible for my spirit.

Forgive me in advance if this acknowledgment runs on for a page or two or . . . three. It's my first book, after all. Authors who have produced ten or twenty books have a chance to thank everyone by book five—or ten. By their twentieth or thirtieth book, however, they are thanking their pet Abyssinian cat, the koi in their backyard pond and maybe the raspberry bushes. After all, how often can you thank your wife/husband, editor/agent, best friends, inspirational sources, etc.? But this is my first acknowl-edgement, and I have a lot of people places and things to give thanks to. But no cats or fish will be here, even though I/we have plenty of them.

First of all, I want to thank my parents, grandparents, great-grandparents, great-great- grandparents—all my ancestors down through the ages. I am their child, the out-flowing of many who struggled to carve out a living on this planet and leave behind offspring, one of whom is me. I especially thank my father, Bob Cole and my mom, Dayle

Nelson, and those that came before them . . . the Coles, Nelsons, Thorsens, Spindlers, Waltons, Wigers, Shockleys, McKees, McNabs, Lees, and the others whose DNA I carry from Norway, Scotland, Ireland, Germany, England and beyond. I stand on their shoulders, reap what they worked hard to build.

In addition to creating me, I want to thank my parents, and especially my father for his career with Kaiser Aluminum. Through this work he chose to transfer to the Bay Area of California and later to West Germany where we lived for five years. My mom and dad took my sister, Cheryl, and I through much of Europe, seeing many places where big history took place, some glorious, some tragic, but almost always fascinating, and educational for my mind, my heart, my soul. This time broadened my perspective, helped me see life from a global and long-term historical view. My father's work was a sacrifice for him at times, as he earned a living that was not of his deepest dreams. His internal conflicts played out in our family at times, with predictable results.

Over the years I've had many teachers, direct and indirect, as learning is everywhere. These teachers, some wise and some not, include the Jehovah Witnesses from my high school, John Traynor, Robert Beamish, Joseph Campbell, Elaine Pages, Unity Church, Redhawk, Bishop Spong, two ex-wives Laurie and Kathleen, the founders of the human potential movement like Ram Dass and Michael Murphy, Uncle Craig and Aunt Doria, and the young men at Phi Kappa Theta. There are too many to name—the preceding list just scratches the surface

I've read many good works of fiction, authors who opened my mind to new possibilities, while entertaining and helping me to enter a new world. My favorites include Charles Dickens, James Michener, Frank Herbert, Orson Scott Card, Richard Brautigan, Terry Brooks, Issac Asimov, Herman Hesse, Ursula LeGuin, Richard Bach, Anne McCaffrey, and more recently Ken Follett, Terry Goodkind, Neil Stephenson, Brent Weeks, and Patrick Rothfuss. It's hard to beat a great story.

One of my greatest teachers has been this incredible, miraculous, and sometimes dangerous planet and vast universe I/we live in and on. I am completely dependent upon the earth for all that I breathe, eat and drink, along with the Sun and to some extent the other "heavenly bodies" which comprise our solar system. And this human body I live in is pretty miraculous, too, incredibly complex, resilient in many ways and fragile in others. I try to keep any abuse to it to a minimum as I am I actuality renting this "space."

Thanks also goes to a few people who I've shared that I was writing this novel. I'm grateful for those who pushed me, encouraged me, asked (year after year) "how the book was coming." In the early days it was Craig Schwandt and Scott Valentine, and over the past dozen years Luke Zarecor and Rebecca Devine, and lately my pastor/mystic/friend Redhawk.

Excellent teachers have also resided at the various places I have worked and/or volunteered for: colleagues, bosses, staffers. From Kaiser to KXLY, INMEN to the WSCPA, Unity Church to STAGE, Arthur/Ernst & Young to EWU, I've been fortunate to have worked with a lot of wise souls.

I received specific, editorial help from several people. Stacie Wachholz was my first copy editor, and she provided me invaluable feedback, and improved this work in a real way. Terry Trueman has been my de-facto editor—and will get his own paragraph in just a little bit. Neil Clemons designed the beautiful cover and Rusty Lynd drew the superb map. Finally, Russ Davis of Gray Dog Press also fulfilled an integral role, providing the vital printing press and e-book uploading knowledge and logistics that is allowing you to read this work.

I've had some really great, long-time friends. Some date back to high school, like Dave Cook, Brian Brown and Greg Doughty. One more friend, Jeff Richards, I met at college. All four helped me survive those tumultuous years. Dave, a fellow mystic and incredible soul, gave up his body ten years ago, but his spirit lives on. I miss him, though, and I wish that he was here to read this book, now that it is finally finished. I'm thankful for these friends; they've been a rich blessing.

Along with those friends above, over the past twenty-five years I've been quite fortunate to know a special group of men. Gene Dire, Michael Gurian, and Terry Trueman and I formed a men's support group in the early 1990's, where we listened to one another, challenged each other and over the years came to love one another. I know, that's a stretch for guys, but it is what it is.

Gene is the quietest one of us, a father of two, working with Catholic Charities to help the poor, the hungry, the down and forgotten. He is a man with a huge heart, deep compassion, and wonderful listening skills. Gene is a true gem.

Special thanks goes to Michael Gurian, a highly talented writer, educator/researcher, counselor and leader, who has shared with our group his successes and tribulations as an author. He's done quite well, with a New York

Times best seller and thirty books in print. A man of many gifts, Michael is also a close spiritual brother and mystic, a fellow traveler through the earthly universe of world religions, and a man who has taught me much during our time together. Michael has been a positive force for good in the world and in my life, and I am grateful to call him friend.

Double special thanks goes to my unofficially adopted big brother Terry, another published author and winner of the Printz Honor Award for his outstanding book Stuck In Neutral. Terry, who admits to being "not well versed" about the genre of this book, nonetheless afforded me invaluable guidance through the writing process. He reviewed and edited my work, suggested the trilogy format, and provided a strong friendship while keeping me humble with his quick wit and biting humor. Terry has also been a force, but the jury is still out if it was for "good" or not. Mostly good for certain, but even he would not want to be known as "all good." I love him like a brother, and he accepts all my quirks (like I accept his), odd humor and inappropriate comments with his mocking grin.

Deep gratitude is owed to my sister, Cheryl (Cole) Barkdull Smith. A blood sister and a spiritual sister, I'm thankful for her friendship, her sisterhood all of these years. Our relationship has always been solid, true, but not always easy, as we both are fiery, intelligent, stubborn seekers of truth. With our parents gone to the next world or back to the earth or to heaven, she helps keep memories alive that only our little nuclear family experienced.

I'm thankful for my wife Debbie, my daughters Jenn and Brie, each who came into my life in a different way and each who have supported me in this long project.

Debbie has always given me the space and time to work on this creation, and is happy that this has finally coming to fruition. Okay, perhaps Debbie is as much relieved, with a deep sigh and a "it's about time" spoken softly. And daughters Jenn and Brie are both wonderful, unique female souls with strong drive and insight. They are finding their own way, their unique path on this planet. I love them in ways I did not know possible when I started this work.

Finally, I owe a tremendous debt of gratitude to the great souls, the mystics, and the sacred texts creators, editors and sustainers. Thank you for your courage, your discipline, your willingness to go where "no one has gone before." You were seeking a connection to that which binds us, transcends us, connects us, gave birth to us and at the end of life collects us—the Almighty, Most High, Ground of Being, Creator, Destroyer, Tao, Allah, Father/ Great Mother/Lord, Higher Power, The One—whatever name you/we wish to give to that which is in many ways—unnamable.

www.ingramcontent.com/pod-product-compliance
Lightning Source LLC
Chambersburg PA
CBHW030307180626
46810CB00003B/955